Hawks Don't
Say Goodbye

Crossway Books by
STEPHEN BLY

THE NATHAN T. RIGGINS
WESTERN ADVENTURE SERIES
(Ages 9–14)

The Dog Who Would Not Smile
Coyote True
You Can Always Trust a Spotted Horse
Last Stubborn Buffalo in Nevada
Never Dance with a Bobcat
Hawks Don't Say Goodbye

THE STUART BRANNON WESTERN SERIES

Hard Winter at Broken Arrow Crossing
False Claims at the Little Stephen Mine
Last Hanging at Paradise Meadows
Standoff at Sunrise Creek
Final Justice at Adobe Wells
Son of an Arizona Legend

THE CODE OF THE WEST
It's Your Misfortune and None of My Own

Hawks Don't Say Goodbye

Stephen Bly

CROSSWAY BOOKS • WHEATON, ILLINOIS
A DIVISION OF GOOD NEWS PUBLISHERS

Hawks Don't Say Goodbye

Copyright © 1994 by Stephen Bly

Published by Crossway Books
       a division of Good News Publishers
       1300 Crescent Street
       Wheaton, Illinois 60187

Cover illustration: David Yorke

First printing, 1994

Printed in the United States of America

Library of Congress Cataloging-in-Publication Data
Bly, Stephen A., 1944-
    Hawks don't say goodbye / Stephen Bly.
      p.   cm.
      1. Frontier and pioneer life—Nevada—Fiction 2. Nevada—Fiction
I. Title. II. Series: Bly, Stephen A., 1944- Nathan T. Riggins western
adventure series; bk. 6.
PZ7.B6275Haw 1994   [Fic]—dc20   94-20255
ISBN 0-89107-782-0

02		01		00		99		98		97		96		95		94
16	15	14	13	12	11	10	9	8	7	6	5	4	3	2	1

For
Angela Price
my trail partner
in
Christiansburg,
Virginia

1

"Colin, quick! Head him off! He's coming over by the dry goods!" Nathan shouted, scrambling out from behind a pickle barrel. The unpainted wooden floor was slick from years of heavy use. "No . . . no, there he goes! Leah, he's coming your way. Grab him!"

"With my hands?" Leah gasped. She backed away from the coffee bin and bumped against a string of garlic hanging from the rafter.

Scooting around a stack of ready-made shirts on his hands and knees, Nathan hollered, "Leah, throw your hat on him!"

"Not this hat! I ain't throwin' this hat on no rat." She backed across the room to the glass candy case.

"Mouse," Nathan corrected. "It's only a mouse. Ah, hah! I've got it cornered! Colin, hand me something to clobber it with."

"You mean a broom or perhaps a—"

"Anything! Hurry!" Nathan shouted.

Colin tossed him a pair of rubber galoshes.

Nathan grabbed the overshoes and slammed them down on the fleeing rodent.

"We did it! Another successful hunt."

7

"Well," Leah pouted, "you seem to have more fun chasing rats than you do spendin' time with me."

"Mouse. It's only a mouse, and besides I only do it every other day."

"Young man!" a stern voice scolded from the front counter of the Galena Mercantile. "I believe, Master Riggins, that you are employed here. Are you not?"

"Eh, yes, ma'am," Nathan stammered, standing to his feet with the overshoes in one hand and the mouse in the other.

"Well, then, I hope you see fit to attend to my order, or I'll have to tell Mr. Anderson that you were shooting marbles in the corner when you should have been working."

"Marbles?" Colin choked. "Actually, he was—"

"I'll be right with you, Mrs. Kearny," Nathan interrupted, quickly dropping the dead mouse into the rubber boots and replacing them on the shelf.

It took him about fifteen minutes to gather Mrs. Kearny's supplies and pack them out to her rig. He pulled a tarp over the goods and then lashed them down. Helping Mrs. Kearny into the wagon, Nathan untied the team and brought her the lead line.

"Thank you, Nathan. Tell Mr. Anderson I'm sorry he wasn't here so that I might say goodbye," she added, pushing her floppy green hat back out of her eyes.

"Goodbye? Are you pulling out?" Nathan asked shading his eyes from the noontime sun.

"Yes. I'm afraid Henry has the wanderin' fever. His brother's raising cherries in California, and Henry's decided what with the Shiloh cutting back, we're going to become cherry farmers."

"Well, ma'am, I'm, eh . . . sorry to see you go." He waved

to her as she slapped the reins and rolled the rig down the street, each wheel leaving a cloud of dry yellow dust.

Leah and Colin were lounging on a bench in front of the store by the time he stepped back up on the raised wooden sidewalk. He unbuttoned the sleeves of his shirt and rolled them halfway up his forearms.

The hot Nevada sun blistered his face, and he squinted his eyes until he reached the cover of shade. Plopping down on the bench next to Leah, he grinned.

"Sure is a pretty hat, Miss Leah."

"Oh . . . sure, I'll bet you say that to all the other girls, too."

"What other girls?" Nathan kidded.

"Riggins, look down Main Street." Colin pointed. "What do you see?"

Nathan wiped the sweat off his forehead and stared down the street. A couple of horses stood tied at the Drover's Cafe. There was a broken buckboard parked in front of the Paradise Dance Hall, which had been closed since November. And he spotted old Ezree Mullins asleep on a bench beside the Welsh Miners' Hall.

"Eh . . . I don't see anything. I mean, it just looks like Galena, Nevada," he answered.

"Precisely!" Colin proclaimed. "That proves what I've been saying all along."

"Do you know what he's talking about?" Nathan asked Leah.

"Me? I never know what Colin's talkin' about. He came with you."

"With me?" Nathan teased, "I thought he came with you."

9

"If you two are quite finished, what I'm talking about," Colin Maddison (with two *d*'s), Jr., explained, "is that this town is absolutely dying!"

"Oh, it's just been a slow summer. I hear they might have found some color up on Crazy Woman Mountain. If they did, then—"

"Riggins, you sound like Henderson down at the post office and the miners sitting unemployed in front of the Miners' Hall! Take a good look. Does this look like the town you arrived at two years ago?"

Nathan glanced at the businesses along Main Street again. At least half of them were boarded up.

"Well, it's just a slump. These things happen, but we'll pull out of it. My dad says—"

"Your dad's a great marshal," Colin acknowledged, "but he isn't a businessman. The town's dying, and now's the time to exit. There's no use waiting until everyone goes broke."

"Come on, Colin, it's not that bad," Nathan insisted. He pulled off his left boot, straightened his sock, and then yanked it back on. "Sure, it's a slow summer, but that doesn't mean we'll dry up and disappear like Willow Springs or something. The cattle froze out last winter, and some of the big ranches shut down, but they'll be back. I've heard some folks say they enjoyed not having the town shot up every Saturday night."

"I don't know, Riggins." Colin pulled out a small folding knife and began to clean his fingernails. "Miss D'Imperio said if five more kids don't come to town this summer to make up for those that have moved, we won't have school in September."

"They'll move in. You'll see," Nathan encouraged him.

"I've been praying that the Lord would move some large families into Galena."

"Oh, like them Rialto sisters, I'll bet. You been prayin' that all seven of them will move to town, have you?" Leah accused.

"No, but that's not a bad idea. Why, I'll bet they look even—"

Leah slugged him in the arm. Nathan tried to avoid the punch and ended up crashing into Colin, knocking him off the bench to the sidewalk.

"Hey, watch it!"

"Sorry, Colin."

Leah scrunched her nose and wrinkled the freckles across her face. "But what if the Lord don't want Galena to go on?" she asked.

"I don't know about your prayers," Colin added, "but I personally happen to know that my father has considered closing the bank."

A shock of alarm shot down Nathan's back. "He can't do that! It's the last bank in town."

"He most certainly can do it. He owns the entire bank, you know."

"Yeah, we know it," Nathan moaned.

"What would your daddy do for a livin'?" Leah asked. "I mean, if he didn't have the bank? Jobs in town is kind of hard to find."

"Why, we'd move to another town and open another bank," Colin explained. "You don't think we'd want to stay here, do you? Father mentioned opening a bank over in White Pine County perhaps."

"I like it here," Leah said softly. "This is the best place I ever lived in my whole life. You ain't goin' to move, are you, Nathan?"

"Nope, not us. 'Course it has been a little tougher since they only pay Daddy part salary. He was saving up to buy a ranch, but now it looks like we've been using some of that savings just to get by on."

"Oh, come on, you two, it ain't the end of the world! It's just a lazy July day, that's all," Leah insisted. "By September folks will be linin' the streets, and we'll wish they would all move on. It's happened before."

Nathan stood to his feet and stepped to the edge of the sidewalk. "Well, Colin's right about one thing. Two years ago there were freight wagons parked three deep and lined back out to old man Blanchard's place. You were lucky if you could cram into a cafe for a meal. Now you're lucky to find a cafe open. Look at the Mercantile. Remember when they had eight clerks working here? Now it's me, Tony, and Mr. Anderson."

Leah jumped to her feet and twirled on the sidewalk. "Well, I don't have to listen to all of this bad talkin'. I'll see you after work . . . I mean, if that's all right with you."

"I'll come by your house," Nathan promised.

She smoothed her long cotton dress with the rich brown velvet bows on the shoulders and hiked off toward her father's barber shop.

Nathan stood in the doorway and watched her walk away.

"Towns do die out here, don't they, Nathan?"

"Yeah . . ." He nodded at Colin. "They can dry up and completely disappear."

"You know, my grandparents live in Boston," Colin remarked. "They've lived in that two-story white house for over fifty-three years. And I suppose someday my uncle and then my cousins will live there too. But out here nothing stays the same very long, does it?"

"I reckon not." Nathan retreated to the doorway of the store. "I sure can't imagine Galena being around fifty years from now."

"Precisely."

"Are you comin' inside?" Nathan asked, running his hand along the rough, unpainted door jamb.

"I think I'll go home and pour a bucket of well water over my head," Colin reported.

"Really?"

"Of course not. It's just a saying when it gets so hot. Nobody actually pours water over their head," Colin explained. He turned to cross the street.

"I do," Nathan muttered under his breath, entering the Mercantile. The comfortable, familiar mixed smells of freshly ground coffee, peppermint stick candy, and new leather greeted him.

Lord, this is not the way I had things planned, remember? I asked You about that ranch and cattle, and when we're older, You know . . . me and Leah. And Colin would be the banker. But now everything's up in the air. Everyone's moving or worried. Nobody in town laughs anymore.

His thoughts were interrupted by Miss Phillips and another woman entering the store.

"Can I fill an order for you ladies?" Nathan asked.

"Why, young Mr. Riggins. I see Mr. Anderson has left you in charge today."

"Only until after he has his dinner," Nathan reported.

"Well, this is my sister, Mrs. Krause, from Charlotte County, Virginia."

"Howdy, ma'am." Nathan nodded. "Pleased to meet you. Are you plannin' on movin' to Galena?"

"Oh, my word, no!" she exclaimed.

"I'm afraid my sister could never leave Virginia," Miss Phillips reported. "Nathan here is the marshal's son. Did I mention Marshal Riggins, Delia? He's a very fine Christian man, you know. Anyway, we're going down to the river tomorrow to escape this dreadful heat, so we thought we'd do a little shopping today. Don't mind us, Nathan. We'll signal if we need some help. We'll just poke around. Maybe over there in the barrel of parasols."

"Yes, ma'am . . . eh, nice to meet you, Mrs. Krause." He smiled and went back to the counter where he began to uncrate some enamel-coated tin dishes.

"My, such a polite young man," he heard Mrs. Krause murmur.

You see, Lord, I like it out here. It's kind of scary not knowin' where you're going to be living. Everyone has to be somewhere and, well . . . this is where I want to be. It's . . . it's comfortable—like an old pair of boots. And it's so quiet and peaceful. It's the kind of place—

A piercing scream shredded his thoughts. He dropped a stack of tin plates.

"A rat! There's a rat in the boots!" Miss Phillips shouted, and she struggled to hold up her trembling sister.

Running to the women, Nathan grabbed up the rubber galoshes and jammed his hand into the boot. He clutched the dead mouse, jerked it out, and scurried to the back door. "I'm really sorry, Miss Phillips. I'll get rid of it right now."

"My word," Mrs. Krause gasped, "did that young man grab that rodent with his bare hands?"

"The children grow up rather leathery out here, don't they?" Miss Phillips brushed down her sleeves and then called out to Nathan, "Mr. Anderson should get a mouser!"

"Yes, ma'am, I'll mention it to him." He dumped the mouse on the dirt beside the back door and then turned a small empty nail barrel over the top of the animal.

By the time he finished waiting on Miss Phillips and her sister, they had both regained their composure and were so busy chattering that they almost walked out the door forgetting their purchases.

"Miss Phillips, your bundle," he called.

"Oh, my heavens . . . yes." She smiled. "Please tell your mother I said hello."

"Yes, ma'am. Thank you."

Nathan finished unpacking and stacking all the tin dishes without another customer entering the store. For several minutes he stood in front of a floor-length mirror and tried on several new hats that he had unboxed earlier in the day.

You're too skinny, Riggins. You grew too fast this year. It's all right to be five feet, ten inches, but you need some girth. Mom's right. I need my hair cut. If Mr. Walker's not too busy, I could get it cut when I stop by and see Leah. Look at this one! Nathan T. Riggins, riverboat gambler. No . . . this is it. This black one. Riggins, you dog, you could be mistaken for . . . for Stuart Brannon himself!

Pretending to be the famous gunman, he sauntered up to the mirror wearing the black hat. "Excuse me, Miss, I'll just mosey on out to the street and face down them fourteen desperados. Then I'll be back and finish my pie."

Glancing at the clock on the wall, he put the hat back on the shelf and walked over to the cash drawer.

Harris Anderson returned to the Mercantile at exactly 1:00 P.M. He looked at his pocket watch, listened to the wall clock chime once, and examined the cash drawer.

"Looks like you had some cash sales. That's a good sign. Go grab yourself some dinner, Nate. You can finish putting up stock later."

Nathan pulled off his heavy ducking apron, hung it on a peg by the back door, shoved on his floppy gray hat, then stepped outside, moved the barrel, and picked up the dead mouse. He ambled down the alley behind the buildings and turned up the hill to the boarded-up Heartford Hotel.

Shading his eyes with his hat, he strained to focus on the roof line of the hotel.

"All right, Domingo . . . I see you up there!"

Nathan reached to his back pocket and pulled out a heavy, worn leather glove and slipped it on his left hand. The gauntlet extended almost to his elbow. Then he held his arm straight out in front of him and let go with a shrill whistle.

"Come on, Domingo! Come on, boy . . . it's dinner time."

Nathan watched for a few moments until the large, brown-winged bird swooped down off the shingles of the hotel and glided to a rest on Nathan's gloved hand.

"I don't know how you do it. How do you have such a soft landing? You're a big boy, but you always feel so light. Have you had a lot to eat today? I hope you aren't too full for a mouse meal. Are you ready?"

The brown hawk swiveled its neck and stared at Nathan, then swiveled back and looked down the street. Nathan could tell he was about ready to fly away.

"Wait . . . wait. Here it comes!"

With his right hand, he tossed the dead mouse high into the air. He felt the hawk kick free from the perch and flap his wide wings. Nathan could hear the beating sound and feel the breeze they made as the powerful bird winged towards the tumbling rodent. The bird's talons snatched the mouse in midair, and with several long flaps of the wings the bird returned to its perch on top of the building.

"Yeah . . . well, you used to come back and say thanks," Nathan called. "That's a big dinner, so I won't be back tomorrow."

He's going away, too, isn't he, Lord? When it gets cold, he'll be gone. Off to someplace sunny. Off to someplace where there's a lonesome lady hawk.

Nathan strolled home thinking about the day he had found the baby hawk in the hayloft above Onepenny's stall. First, the bird nested in a coffee can half full of straw, then in an empty nail barrel, then in the abandoned chicken coop, and finally Nathan had turned him loose and found that Domingo preferred the roof of the Heartford Hotel.

Walking across the dirt yard in front of his house, Nathan was greeted by a tail-wagging, limping gray and white dog.

"Tona, you don't have to come out in the sun. Stay back there and rest up. You're all stove-up today, aren't you, old boy?" He rubbed the dog's ears and scratched its head. The dog sniffed him up one arm and down the other.

"It's a mouse. You smell it, don't you? It's okay, don't worry. I fed him to Domingo."

The dog struggled back into the shade of the porch and flopped down on a small, worn braided rug that had become

17

his permanent dwelling place ever since Nathan brought him back from the Rialto ranch early in the spring.

He washed his hands in a basin on the porch.

"Nate," his mother called, "bring in a couple more sticks of wood for the cookstove."

On entering the kitchen, he heard the sound of meat frying and crackling in the skillet, and he smelled the aroma of ham.

"How was work this morning, dear?" she asked, pouring herself a cup of coffee.

"Really slow," he reported. "It's like everyone's out of town today. Oh, Miss Phillips came in and said to tell you hello. Did you know her sister came to visit her?"

"Came to help her move, I hear," Nathan's mother responded.

"Move? Miss Phillips is moving from Galena?"

"So I hear."

"Did you know the Kearnys are leaving too?"

"No. Where did you hear that?"

"Mrs. Kearny told me herself. You know, Mom, town will perk up next fall, and all these people are going to regret cashing in so quickly," Nathan reported.

"Well, I certainly hope so." His mother set a bowl of boiled potatoes on the table and then forked the sizzling meat onto their plates.

"Where's Dad?"

"He went to Austin."

Nathan sat up straight. "Austin? He didn't tell me he was going! What's he doing in Austin?"

"Looking for a job."

"A job? He has a job!"

"Well, not any more." His mother sighed.

With a chunk of ham only inches from his mouth, Nathan's head swung up with surprise. "What?"

"The mayor stopped by and said they can't afford to pay him anymore, what with everyone leavin'. So they are going to have to call a posse whenever the need arises."

"But . . . but he's just got to be marshal!" Nathan protested. "This whole town's going crazy. I don't get it. Why's everyone leavin'?"

"I suppose, Nathan T. Riggins, that they all like to eat, too."

2

Nathan's afternoon blurred as he stocked shelves and waited on customers at the Galena Mercantile. His mind kept racing over the idea that his family might soon be one of those to leave Galena. It hung like a drooping hat over his head even as he entered Walker's Barber Shop several hours later.

"Hi, Mr. Walker. You got any time for a haircut?"

Leah's father looked up from a newspaper and glanced at his otherwise empty shop.

"Time? Nathan, I have time to cut hair for the entire U. S. army. Hop in the chair, and I'll give you a trim."

"Thanks. Is Leah at home?"

"Well, son, if she's not with you, chances are mighty good she's upstairs, but I ain't seen her since dinner."

"Sure is a quiet summer, isn't it?" Nathan mentioned as Mr. Walker strapped his scissors.

"Quiet? Nearly dead, I figure. If things don't perk up this fall, I don't suppose there will be many left that winter out."

"How about you, Mr. Walker?"

"Well, Nate . . . a man's got to go where there's customers. And lately I haven't been cuttin' much hair or pullin' many teeth, that's for sure. I've thought about takin' a look at Silver City."

20

"In Idaho?"

"Yep."

"Isn't that where that Kylie Collins guy is?" Nathan asked.

"Well, I reckon you're right."

"I ain't goin' to no Silver City!" a voice boomed from the back door.

"Leah!" Nathan blurted out.

"Daddy, I told you I made up my mind. I ain't ever goin' to marry that Kylie Collins. I think we should stay in Galena as long as . . . well . . . you know."

Nathan watched in the big mirror as Mr. Walker ran a comb though his dark brown hair and clipped it shorter. "As long as that good-lookin' Riggins boy lives here. Was that what you were goin' to say?"

"Daddy!"

"Now, Nate, let me tell you about this Leah-girl. She's sort of like those Gila monsters down in Arizona. Have you ever seen them?"

"Eh . . . no, sir."

"Well, they're nothing but a huge fat lizard. Some grow to two or three feet. Anyway, when they get mad and lock their teeth into you, they never let go. You got to literally hack them to pieces with your huntin' knife to get them to turn loose. Now ol' Leah-girl . . . she's clamped her iron will down on Mr. Nathan T. Riggins. I'm afraid you don't have much chance of ever gettin' loose."

"Daddy! I ain't goin' to stand here and be humiliated. Supper's ready if you're hungry, and Nathan can stay if he wants to." Leah turned to leave.

"Eh . . . I, eh, you know . . . need to check with my mother. With Dad gone, she might not want to be alone."

"She ain't alone," Leah offered.

"What do you mean?"

"She's upstairs at the supper table waitin' for us."

"What? She didn't tell me that we were havin' supper over here."

"Well, that just goes to show you don't know everything, Mr. Nathan T. Riggins!" Leah turned and scampered out the back door of the barber shop.

"There you have it, Nate—one very opinionated young lady."

Nathan swallowed a lump in his throat. "Mr. Walker, Leah sure is a good friend for me. I really do like her."

"Son, I appreciate you sayin' that. 'Cause that little lady thinks the sun rises and sets with Nathan T. Riggins."

Nathan was afraid to glance in the mirror. He knew his face would be burning.

"Your daddy out chasing outlaws?" Mr. Walker asked.

"Eh . . . no, he's . . . he's down in Austin."

"Had to go to the courthouse, huh?"

"Well . . . maybe. I mean . . . actually, Mr. Walker, they laid him off as marshal. Said they couldn't afford a lawman anymore. So Dad's down in Austin lookin' for a job or some-thing."

"You don't say! I didn't know." Mr. Walker brushed Nathan off and sprinkled some talc on the back of his neck. "Well, this is . . . it surely does cause a man to consider driftin' on out."

Nathan handed Mr. Walker a quarter.

"Oh, no, it's my treat, what with your daddy being out of work and—"

"No, sir, Mr. Walker!" Nathan insisted. "I'm still workin'. Besides, my mama would skin me alive if I didn't pay my own way."

The barber glanced at Nathan, then smiled, and took the quarter. "You got good folks, Nathan. I hope you remember to thank the Lord for 'em."

"Every night." Nathan nodded.

"Well, I'm closing up and sweeping the shop. Tell the ladies I'll be right up."

"Yes, sir, I will."

■

The following day Nathan didn't have to go to work until 1:00 P.M., so he saddled up Onepenny at the first sign of daylight. Then he slid his carbine into its scabbard, put some biscuits into his saddlebags, and strapped his canteen over the saddle horn.

Tona limped out into the middle of the dirt yard to watch him.

"You want to go, boy? You can't keep up anymore. You know that." He stared at the sad face that seemed to be Tona's permanent expression.

"Okay." Nathan shrugged. "Come on . . . Onepenny can carry us both. He'll like some company." Lifting the crippled animal, Nathan struggled to climb into his saddle and situate the dog in his lap.

"All right, gang. Let's go huntin'."

They rode down Main Street without seeing any sign of

life. The July air was dry, still, and already losing any coolness the night might have brought. An aroma of dust and sage hung heavy about them.

In a little over an hour, they had swooped down through the valley, crossed Lewis Creek, and begun to climb up into the Shoshone Mountains. He finally left the barren hills and hit the chaparral at Rabbit Springs where he climbed off Onepenny. He loosened the cinch and hobbled the spotted horse to graze on what little grass was near the pool of water.

Tona slumped over to the shade of a scrub cedar, circled three times, and then lay down where he could watch the horse and the springs.

Nathan stared at his dog.

Lord, Tona hurts all the time. I kept prayin' all last summer that he'd live after that bobcat tore him up. And You answered my prayers, but . . . maybe it wasn't so good an idea. He can't hunt. He can't run. He can hardly watch over me. Lord, either let him regain his strength, or . . . or, You know . . . well, I just can't watch him hurt so bad every day.

His canteen strapped around his neck, his Winchester carbine in his left hand and two biscuits in his right, Nathan hiked up the mountain past the piñon pines on the north side of the slope. Reaching a jagged row of rocks above the tree line, he sat where he could look to the east, west, and north.

Munching on the biscuits, he watched the horizon for any sign of the pronghorn antelopes that he'd seen several weeks earlier.

Lord, well, I'd like to shoot an antelope and show Mom and Dad I can contribute to the food supply. But really I guess I rode out here to think a little bit. All I ever wanted was to be with Mom and Dad. I remember how I wandered around this country two years ago lookin' for them. I said then if I found them, that's all I would ever ask for.

But this time it seems different. I've got friends . . . good friends like Colin and Leah. I don't want us to all move away. When I get old, I want to be able to say to someone, "Remember when we were kids?"

It's crazy out here, Lord. Everyone's in a hurry to get rich . . . they run to Virginia City . . . they run to Bodie . . . they run to Eureka . . . they run to Belmont. You can live your whole life and never get to know anybody at all. It's like you're always visitin' . . . never stayin'.

Someday, Lord, someday I'm goin' to buy me a ranch and never ever move. My kids will spend their whole life in that same house, no matter what.

I mean, if Leah doesn't mind.

Sudden movement caused Nathan to jerk his head to the right and lift his carbine to his shoulder. Trailing the metal sights of the gun across the horizon, he followed the dust of what looked like several animals running at the lower edge of the chaparral. He lowered the weapon and continued to watch until they dropped over the western horizon of the mountain.

A rifle with a Vernier sight maybe, but not with a carbine—not at this distance. Last week they ran up on top . . . now they're down there. It's like they always know where I'm going to be.

■

It was over an hour later when Nathan gave up the hunt without firing a shot and hiked back to Rabbit Springs. Tona greeted him with one lone bark. He thumped his tail but didn't bother getting to his feet.

Nathan remounted with Tona and rode back to Galena. It was almost noon when they reached the north/south road and turned up the mountain. The windswept town looked deserted from a distance. There were no rigs on the road, no prospectors' tents scattered about the hillside, no noise from Shiloh's stamp mill. No dogs barked. No children shouted.

As he drew closer, he noticed a number of men talking in front of the bank and several women walking down toward the church.

"Well, Tona, at least it's dying peacefully. Just slowly, a little at a time—nothing painful. Someday we'll just wake up, and no one will be left."

He pulled the tack off Onepenny and turned the spotted horse out in the corral. Then, with Tona tucked under his left arm and his carbine over his right shoulder, he hiked down the back alley to his house. He cradled the dog on its rug and stuck his head through the doorway.

"Mom, I'm home. I didn't have any luck with a pronghorn, but it was a nice ride."

"Do you want some dinner?" she asked.

"Nah. Thanks. I'm stuffed with all your biscuits. I'm going down to the store. Maybe I'll stop and see Colin on the way. Will Dad be in for supper?"

"That all depends on when and where he finds work. He did say he would be home by Saturday, no matter what."

"Good. I want to talk to him."

"About what?"

"About stayin' in Galena rather than moving."

"Nathan, you know we'll have to do what your father thinks best."

"Yes ma'am, but I aim to use my best logic to persuade him to stay."

■

As was his custom, Nathan stayed off Main Street as he tramped over to the Mercantile. Swinging up the hillside, he purposely detoured by the Heartford Hotel.

"Domingo? Did you go off huntin'? You won't be able to eat it, and you know it. You'll come back and hold a mouse for two hours and then drop it down for the cats to find . . . just like last week." He searched the sky, but he couldn't find the hawk anywhere. "Well, I just hope you don't go down to Swifty's chicken coop again. He'll plug you with that shotgun."

He picked up a couple of small rocks and tossed them across the dusty street. Then he trotted down to the back door of the Mercantile.

The door's locked? Am I late? Did Mr. Anderson close for dinner? Where's Tony? He always works the noon hour on Wednesdays.

Scooting around to the front of the store, he noticed a fairly large crowd of people now gathered in front of the bank.

"Hey, what's going on here? What happened?"

"Nathan!" Leah yelled from across the street. "Where have you been?"

They met out in the center of the street.

"Eh . . . I went huntin' in the Shoshones. What's all the fuss?"

"They robbed the bank, that's what!"

"Maddison's bank? Who did it?"

"Nobody knows."

"Did anyone get hurt?"

"Colin's daddy was hit on the head, and Mr. Melton was tied up, but they didn't get shot."

"How about Colin? Was he there?"

"He got locked in the safe."

"In the safe!"

Leah walked with Nathan closer to the crowd. "I heard he was yelling at the outlaws that Marshal David Riggins would chase them down and shoot them dead, and they shoved him into the safe."

"But he's okay now? Right?" Nathan pressed.

A big man who smelled like black powder turned and looked at Nathan. "I hear they can't get the kid out. The dial got jammed when they busted it open."

Nathan pushed through the crowd. "But . . . he'll suffocate in there!"

"That's for sure." The big man nodded.

The crowd ended at the door. Brady Wheeler blocked it with the strength gained from a life of hammering and drilling hard rock.

"Mr. Wheeler, have they got Colin out of the safe?"

"Not yet, Nate. Mr. Maddison's workin' his fingers off tryin'."

"Can we help or anything?"

"Nah, there's nothin' you can—"

"Nathan! Leah! Let them in, Brady!" Mr. Maddison shouted.

They pushed their way into the bank where the smell of gunpowder hung in the air.

"Mr. Maddison, how's Colin? Is he . . . I mean—"

"Nate, the door on the safe is jammed just enough to let a little bit of air inside. Colin will be all right for a while. But the dial is so smashed that we had to send up to the CP and get some equipment for busting it open."

"What can I do?" Nathan asked.

"Talk to him. Just stay with him. He's pretty scared."

"Yes, sir, I'll do it. Who's goin' after the robbers?"

"The mayor said he'd wire the sheriff."

"In Austin?"

"Now that we don't have a marshal, it's about all we can do. Forget the money, Nate. Just help Colin relax and stay calm."

"Yes, sir, I'll stay here as long as I need to." Nathan swung toward the safe and then turned back.

"Leah, can you run over to the Mercantile and tell Mr. Anderson why I'm not coming in? The back door was still locked, so he might be at dinner."

"Until straight up 1:00, right? I'll tell him."

Nathan scooted over to the five-foot door on the safe and found it barely open—not enough to let in much direct light, but enough to allow a little fresh air to filter in.

Holding his ear to the opening of the door, he could hear Colin crying.

"Colin, can you hear me? It's Nate!"

The crying continued.

"Colin, hold on . . . your dad's gone to try and get a fresh air pump from the Shiloh mine. It'll help you breathe easier. You've got to relax. Colin, do you hear me?"

"I am relaxing!" Colin wailed. "I've never . . . been so . . . so relaxed . . . in my life. Get me out of here, Riggins!"

"Listen, Colin, it won't be too long, and I'll stay right here."

"I want my mother! Get my mother!" Colin screamed.

"Your mother's in Carson City, remember?"

"I want out of here! Right now!"

"Colin . . . eh . . . listen, did you get a good look at the bank robbers?" Nathan quizzed.

He heard the sobbing stop.

"Is your father chasing them?" Colin hollered.

"No," Nathan shouted back, "he's down in Austin. But they'll get caught."

"And hung," Colin added.

"Listen, try not to be upset. Just, well, why don't you close your eyes and pretend you're asleep," Nathan suggested. "This will all be just a bad dream."

"And why don't you jump down a mine shaft, Riggins! This is a living nightmare. Get me out of here!"

"Do you want me to sing?" Nathan suggested.

"Get an iron bar and rip open this door!"

"It's too big. Only the Central Pacific has tools that strong."

"Then get the Central Pacific down here immediately. I want my father . . . where's my father?"

"Colin, is there any money left in there?"

"What did you say?"

Nathan leaned over close to the safe's door. "Is there any money in there?"

"How would I know what's in . . . hey . . . hey, Nate!"

"Yeah?"

"I think there's a couple of gold bars back here. Yes, I'm sure of it. Those jerks didn't even find the gold!"

"What else is in there?"

There was a long pause.

"I want out, Riggins. Quit changing the subject."

"You'll be all right, Colin . . . just don't panic."

"Don't panic? Don't panic! Riggins, if I can't panic now, when on earth am I allowed to panic? Why do these things always happen to me?"

He began to bawl again.

"Colin . . . hey . . . what would Stuart Brannon do if he were in there?"

"What?"

"Brannon . . . what would he do?"

Again he stopped crying.

"Brannon would shoot his way out . . . no, he'd pick the lock with his penknife."

"Brannon doesn't carry a penknife," Nathan yelled.

Leah rushed up to him. "Nathan! Hey, no one's over at the Mercantile."

"What time is it?"

"It's 1:15, and Mr. Anderson ain't been home for dinner neither. I asked Mrs. Anderson."

"Is the front door locked?"

"Yep."

"I've got to go check it out. Come here and talk to Colin until Mr. Maddison gets back."

"Talk to him? What do I say?"

"Tell him to relax. Tell him that help is on the way. Tell him not to try something dumb and injure himself."

"Colin, this is Leah . . . are you really in there?"

"Where's Nathan?"

"He'll be back."

31

"What are you doing here?"

"The whole town's here." Nathan heard Leah shout as he crashed out the front door and into the brightness of the early afternoon sun.

Pushing through the crowd, he ran to the Mercantile and rattled the front door. He placed his face to the glass and screamed, "Mr. Anderson? Are you in there?"

He heard nothing and started to turn to go back to the bank when he noticed something strange on the floor of the store. With a sudden reckless lunge, he rammed the tall double doors with his shoulder, and they swung open.

"Mr. Anderson!" he hollered, running to the side of a man lying in the aisle between the dry goods and the hardware.

3

Nathan pulled the gag out of Harris Anderson's mouth and fumbled at the ropes that tied the store owner. The hemp burned into his fingers as he tugged at the knot.

"What happened?"

"Three of them . . . they got the jump on me . . . took mainly cash and guns. Tony's tied up in the back room," he panted.

"Must be the ones that robbed the bank," Nathan surmised.

"The bank? They got the bank? Did anyone get hurt?"

"Eh . . . well . . ." Nathan hesitated. "No one's in too bad a shape. I mean, no one got shot. You all right? Should I go find the doc?"

"Nate, I'll take care of Tony. Is your daddy still down at the county seat?"

"Yes, sir. He's in Austin."

"Lettin' him go was the dumbest thing this town ever did!"

"The mayor said he wired Austin about the bank, so I guess the sheriff will be coming up. I'll go tell them about the Mercantile."

"Nate, go up and down Main Street and see that no one else has been robbed also."

"Yes, sir . . . eh, Mr. Anderson, is it all right if I don't work today? Colin's stuck in the safe at the bank, and I promised to stay with him until they get him out."

"Stuck in the safe? How in the world did he—"

"Eh . . . it's just the kind of thing that only Colin can do," Nathan reported.

"Listen, stop by in the morning. I'm goin' to close up and take inventory to see what else might be missing. Then I'll stir up a crew of men and see if we can find some tracks before the wind blows them all to Utah."

■

Nathan passed word of the holdups to all the other businesses. None had been aware of the robberies.

Then he returned to the bank. Mr. Maddison and Brady Wheeler were unbolting the back of the safe from the stone wall. Leah stared in fascination, twirling her brown hair on her finger.

"Mr. Maddison, what are you doing?" Nathan inquired.

"The Central Pacific telegraphed and said the only tools that could do the job were fastened to a mail car in Battle Mountain Station. If we get the safe to them, we can use the tools."

"You're goin' to take the whole safe to Battle Mountain?"

"Yes, it seems to be our only choice."

"Can you lift this thing? I mean, what freight wagon can hold it?"

"How about Abel Mercee's Buffalo Tight #1?" Leah shouted.

Nathan's eyes lit up. "Thunder's wagon? Sure!"

"Is it still around?" Mr. Maddison asked.

"Yeah, but it will be rusted. Mr. Mercee left it here when he moved to Bisbee," Nathan reported.

"Brady, I'll finish this up. Go see if you can get that wagon in rolling shape," Mr. Maddison commanded.

"Should I go help him?" Nathan asked.

"No . . . no. You talk to Colin. Keep talking to him."

Trying to stay out of the others' way, Nathan crawled up by the safe door and shouted into the crack.

"Colin! It's me, Nathan. They robbed the Mercantile, too!"

"Did anyone catch them yet? Don't let them hang them until I get out. I want to see them hang."

"No," Nathan hollered, "they haven't been caught. What did they look like?"

"Mean!"

"What?"

"They were mean-looking—bandannas, guns, dirty hats, tobacco stains on their vest . . . you know the type."

"Colin, did you know we're taking the safe to Battle Mountain Station?"

"Yeah, but . . ."

Nathan could hear Colin begin to cry.

"What is it? Colin?"

"I'll die in this steel box out in that heat!" he sobbed.

"Tell him we're not going until after dark," Mr. Maddison reported as he pulled the last bolt from the wall.

"Colin . . . we aren't going until after dark."

"What if the wagon breaks down? What if we're stranded? I'll bake like a turkey!" he moaned.

"It won't happen . . . we'll get you there," Nathan assured him.

"Are you going with us?" Colin hollered.

"I'll be there. Now sit still! They're going to try and pull the safe off the wall."

"Don't let the door close all the way," he shouted.

"It's all fixed. Don't worry about that."

"Nathan!"

"Yeah?"

"I'm hungry!"

"That's good . . . that's good, Colin."

"Why?"

"'Cause you're thinking about something other than this lousy safe."

■

Nathan spent the rest of the afternoon at the bank next to the safe. About 4:00 P.M., Leah brought him a loaf of fresh-baked bread, some slices of roast beef, and a bowl of boiled turnips and cabbage, which he ate quickly.

Nathan was reading a book to Colin entitled *Stuart Brannon and the Argentine Outlaws* by Hawthorne H. Miller when Brady Wheeler came in and announced it was time to load up.

"Did you tell my mother what's going on?" Nathan asked Leah.

"Yeah, she sent your coat, your canteen, and your carbine. She said to be careful and tell ya she was prayin' for you and for Colin."

Praying? Lord, how come I haven't been praying? Please keep Colin alive . . . You've got to help him!

"Listen, we should be back tomorrow afternoon. Could you tell Mr. Anderson what I'm doing, and, well, could you take some . . . meat scraps and—"

"And feed that chicken-killing vulture?"

"Domingo's a hawk. Just toss the meat up into the air. He'll come get it. Please? He needs to eat every other day."

"Oh, all right." Leah sighed. "Nathan?"

"Yeah?"

"I'll be prayin' for you and Colin, too."

"Thanks."

"Nathan!" a muffled voice shouted.

"It's all right, Colin . . . they're going to load you up now."

■

The evening sun had dropped behind the western hills when the safe was loaded by eight strong men into Abel Mercee's Buffalo Tight #1 wagon. A six-up team of mules led the way with Brady Wheeler driving. Mr. Maddison sat next to Nathan in the back of the wagon, which no longer sported a tailgate. Two other men rode horses behind.

"It's getting darker in here, Nathan!" Colin shouted.

"It's gettin' darker out here, too. Maybe you can get some sleep."

"No!" Colin shouted. "I won't sleep . . . I can't sleep."

"How come?"

"'Cause I'm afraid I won't wake up," he sobbed.

Nathan reached over and spun the broken dial on the safe. It twirled free like nothing was happening on the inside.

"What are you doing?" Colin yelled.

"Just twisting the dial. You want me to stop?"

"No . . . no! Keep it up. Then I know you're really out there."

For the next two hours Nathan and Mr. Maddison took turns talking to Colin and spinning the dial on the safe. Sometime after the sixth time Mr. Maddison sang through "Amazing Grace," Nathan nodded off.

He dreamed about sitting on top of the Heartford Hotel and watching three men rob the bank. But instead of riding horses to get away, they rode pigs. Huge, ugly, long-tusked, wild pigs.

"Nate." Mr. Maddison poked him. "Can you take a spell? I keep dozing off."

"Oh . . . yes, sir . . . is Colin asleep?"

"I'm not asleep, Riggins. I happen to be starving to death! Are you out there? How come you're not twisting that dial? Are you eating? I can smell ham. Maybe you could slip a slice of . . . a really thin slice of ham in here! Nathan? Are you there?"

Nathan's voice was hoarse, and every bone in his body ached for sleep as the wagon creaked its way up the Battle Mountain Station road. One of the outriders had switched with Brady Wheeler to drive the rig, and Nathan could whiff the smell of tobacco in the man's pipe. The summer night sky, painted with stars, seemed much brighter with the absence of a moon.

Suddenly he stopped twisting the dial as the heavy metal object fell like a brick into his hand.

"Hey!" he yelped. "It broke!"

"Nathan?" Colin called. "I don't hear you twisting the dial. Nathan!"

"I'm here, Colin. The thing broke. I'm sorry, but the dial broke off—or something."

"What do you mean it broke? It can't break."

"I didn't mean to do it. It just fell off in my hand, that's all. Listen, I'll tap on the safe."

"Nathan, is there a hole in the safe where the dial was?" Colin asked.

Nathan probed in the darkness with his hand. "Yeah . . . but, I mean, there's another metal plate. It doesn't go clear through," he reported to Colin.

"I know that. Now reach in there and see if you can feel a steel rod."

"A rod? What do you mean, a rod?"

"You know . . . about the size of your thumb. It should be sticking out where the dial used to be, but pointing to the right."

"Yeah," Nathan hollered. "I found it. Now what?"

"Pull it."

"Pull it? What do you mean, pull it?"

"Pull it in the direction it's pointing. Pull it, Nathan!"

"I can't pull it! It doesn't budge, Colin."

"Wait, Nathan! Wait until I wiggle the door. When I'm wiggling the door, you pull the rod."

"Hey! It's moving, Colin! Keep shoving the door . . . yeah, it's moving."

"Nate?" Mr. Maddison shook himself awake and stood up at the back of the rambling iron wagon. "What's happening?"

With a tandem effort, Nathan shoved the rod another inch just as Colin thrust at the door. Suddenly the heavy safe door swung open, catching Mr. Maddison in the chest as he started to stand up.

"It's open!" Colin shouted, gasping for fresh air.

Stumbling, trying to catch his balance, Mr. Maddison shoved the door away from him. The heavy door crashed closed. And Mr. Maddison tumbled off the back of the wagon.

The driver, who had been half asleep, reined up the team, and the outriders trotted up.

"What's goin' on?"

"Maddison's on the ground."

"We had it open. The door was open!" Nathan cried. He heard kicking from inside the safe, and immediately he grabbed the pin and shoved it to the right. Once again the door flew open. This time Colin dove out into the night, rolled off the back of the wagon, and crashed into his father who was being helped to his feet. Both plunged full-spraddle onto the packed dirt roadway.

For fifteen minutes shouts, hugs, tears, and an occasional joyous gunshot filled the night air like a Fourth of July celebration in a gold camp.

An hour later, the wagon was well on its way back to Galena. Nathan and Colin sat side by side next to Mr. Maddison who was driving. Colin's hands still trembled as he clutched Nathan's canteen in his lap.

"I can't believe you didn't bring any food! You could have starved to death out here. What if you took a wrong turn and got lost?"

"There aren't any turns on this road," Nathan replied.

"Well . . . there could have been a storm. If a blizzard

blew in and all of you were stranded, what would you eat? My word, you've got to think about these things!"

"Colin, it's July! We won't get a blizzard. Besides, we'll get back to Galena before daylight."

"I haven't eaten since breakfast, and I can't get my mind off food."

"Well," Nathan said searching for an idea, "tell me about . . . eh, safes. How did you know what was inside that dial?"

"I collect them."

"You collect safes?"

"No. I collect books about safes. Companies are always sending catalogs to father, and I collect them. Did you know they once made a safe so heavy that when they placed it aboard ship, the ship sank?"

"Eh . . . no, I didn't know that." Nathan shrugged.

"Well, there's a lot of interesting things about safes you don't know, so I'll tell you."

And he did.

Somewhere between the story of a man who kept fake snakes in his safe and daylight, Nathan fell asleep.

■

Galena bustled with confusion when they arrived back in town. The streets streamed with loud, noisy people. Everyone talked of the holdups, but no one seemed to know what to do next.

Except Colin.

He went to the Drover's Cafe, ate two orders of ham, eggs, biscuits, and gravy and then trotted home and went to bed.

Mr. Maddison tried to put some order back into the bank and began to determine how much the thieves had stolen. Down at the Mercantile, Mr. Anderson, although extremely pessimistic, was open for business again. And everyone was demanding that the mayor and the whole city council resign for dismissing Marshal Riggins.

Several men had combed the countryside looking for the outlaws, but they returned without any clues whatsoever. As far as Nathan could determine, no one saw the men enter town, and no one saw them leave. Most figured that the Mercantile was robbed first, but even that was debated. A number of merchants, including Mr. Anderson, threatened to pull out of town if they didn't get better protection.

Nathan filled in Leah and Mr. Walker on the nighttime ride in the former buffalo wagon. He was just leaving to go home when Leah called out, "Your old hawk ain't there, so I threw the scraps to the dogs."

"Domingo isn't there?"

"That's what I said."

"But he knows that I feed him every other day. He wouldn't—"

"Well, he ain't there. Maybe he lost his calendar. He probably flew off to the mountains like all decent hawks ought to."

"He'll be back later. I'll check on him after I get something to eat."

"You goin' to go get some sleep?" she asked.

"Nah. I'm not that tired. I'll probably go see if I can help Mr. Anderson at the Mercantile."

Nathan left the barber shop, cut down the alley beside the closed Oriental Cleaners, and traveled up the back street to his house. Tona performed his ritual of limping halfway across the yard to greet him and then returned to his rug.

Nathan fell asleep between the second helping of potatoes and a double serving of apple cobbler. He sort of noticed his mother leading him off to bed.

■

His father's voice startled him awake. His dad and mother were having a discussion in the kitchen.

"Dad!" Nathan shouted running into the room where his parents sat at the table drinking coffee. "Did you hear about the holdups? And Colin got locked in the—"

The shining badge caught Nathan's attention.

"They made you marshal again?" he asked.

"Nope. I hired on with the county sheriff. I'll be the deputy in charge of this end of the county."

"Can we still live in Galena?"

"For a while. If the town plays out, we might need to move."

"Are you going to catch those outlaws?"

"I'm going to take a look at it, but they've got over a day's head start, and from what I hear, no one has any idea which way they went. Anyway, eat some supper and I'll be back shortly. I've got to catch Mr. Maddison before he and Colin pull out."

Nathan's father yanked on his hat and hurried out the door.

"Supper? Is it that late? Hey, what did Dad mean about Colin pulling out?"

"Mr. Maddison has decided to pay off the depositors the

best he can and shut down the bank. He's leaving Mr. Melton to settle up here. He and Colin are riding up to the Central Pacific and will meet Mrs. Maddison in Carson City."

"They're taking a vacation?"

"I'm not sure they're coming back," his mother replied.

"What do you mean? Just because they were robbed? What if father recovers the money? They aren't leavin' for good, are they?"

His mother came over to the table and rested her hand on Nathan's shoulder. "Well . . . if I were you, I'd skip supper and go talk to Colin."

"Eh . . . yes, ma'am, I mean, is it all right with you?"

"Go on." She nodded.

Nathan ran right down the middle of Main Street and whipped around the corner to Colin's big two-story house. There was a buggy parked out front and several large trunks loaded in the back. The front door of the house stood open.

"Colin!"

"Up here!" came a shout. "Come on up."

Nathan ran up the stairs two at a time and burst into Colin's room. His dark-haired friend stood staring out the window.

"What's all this about leaving? You guys aren't leaving for good . . . are you?" Nathan pleaded.

When he reached the far side of the room, he could see that Colin was crying.

Lord . . . I don't . . . I don't know what to say. Help me not say something dumb.

Suddenly, Nathan began to cry. He tried to stop. He brushed his eyes on the long sleeves of his shirt and blurted out, "Colin, I don't want you to move!"

"I've got to . . . I've got to, Nathan . . . I can't stay."

"But, I mean . . . your dad can . . . he can start a new bank, or open an assay office, or sell mining stock, or work for the Central Pacific."

Colin brushed back his tears and turned to face Nathan. "We lost most of our money in the robbery. Father's been loanin' out a lot, and people have moved off without repaying. We've got just about enough to settle accounts."

"But my dad can catch those robbers. You'll get the money back!" Nathan insisted.

"Maybe, but this town's dying, and Father says now it's time to move."

"Let me talk to him. Maybe I can change his mind," Nathan pleaded.

"It's not just him, Nathan. I want to move, too."

"What? Why?"

"I got real scared in that safe, Nate. No, really, I'm afraid to live here. I want to go somewhere that has policemen and incandescent lights and indoor plumbing . . . I'm scared out here. I've always been scared. Nathan, I've never been brave like you are. You know that. You and Leah tease me about it all the time."

"But we didn't mean anything. Colin, you're my very best friend in the whole world! You can't go!"

"One of your two best friends," he corrected.

"Are you leavin' tonight?"

"We're leaving just as soon as your father gets through talking to mine."

"Couldn't you wait for morning? How about Leah? Does she know you're going?"

"I don't think so."

"Listen, I'm going to go get her. She'll be mad at me if I don't tell her. And you know what she's like if she gets mad."

Colin broke into a smile. "Yeah, go get Leah."

"You won't leave until we get back?"

"I promise."

"Are you sure you can keep your father from pulling out?"

"You've seen me throw a tantrum, haven't you?" Colin grinned.

"You're the best," Nathan teased.

"Thank you." Colin bowed. "Now go get Leah. This is my last valise to pack."

4

Nathan could feel the dust fog up to his face from the pounding of his feet as he ran up Main Street shouting at the top of his voice, "Leah! Leah!"

She bounded down the stairs with one black boot laced up and another in her hands.

"Nathan T. Riggins, you better have a good reason for screamin' at me!" she hollered, flopping down on the bottom worn wooden stair and pulling on her other boot. "What are you hollerin' about anyway?"

"Colin . . . it's Colin!" Nathan panted, bending at the waist to catch his breath.

"He ain't caught in the safe again, is he?"

"No . . . no . . . he's leavin'. Colin's leavin'!"

"Where's he goin'?"

"He's movin', Leah! The Maddisons are moving out of Galena!"

"You mean . . . he won't be here for school or nothin'?"

"School?" Nathan shouted. "He won't be here for breakfast! He's leavin' town right now! Hurry!"

Nathan grabbed Leah by her hand and pulled her out into the street. They began running toward Colin's house.

"I can run jist fine without you holdin' my hand," she puffed, trying to keep up. Nathan started to drop his grip, but

Leah squeezed his hand even tighter. They arrived out of breath and still hand in hand. Colin and his father stood by the loaded carriage talking to Mr. Riggins.

"Are you really leavin' us?" Leah blurted out.

Nathan noticed that Colin had washed his face and now seemed to have regained his composure.

"Well, it was bound to happen. Gold mining camps are so unstable, you know," Colin pronounced.

"I don't want you to move," Leah protested.

"My word, now, you aren't going to get emotional, are you? You see, Riggins? Women just can't handle a goodbye."

Just then Leah threw her arms around Colin's neck, hugged him tight, and kissed him on the cheek. "Well, I'm goin' to really miss you, no matter how snobby you act!"

When she pulled back, Nathan could see Colin's face blush red and tears flood down his cheeks.

"Good heavens," Colin choked, "the dust sure is bad this evening!" He wiped his eyes on his sleeves.

"It's time, Colin," Mr. Maddison called, climbing into the carriage and lifting the reins.

For a moment Nathan and Colin just stared at each other.

"Well," Colin swallowed hard, "you surely aren't going to kiss me, too, are you?"

Nathan threw his arms around Colin's shoulders and hugged him tight. Both boys had tears streaming down their cheeks.

"You got to write to me and tell me where you're living," Nathan demanded.

"I will, I promise."

"And . . . and you'll let me borrow your latest Brannon book," Nathan added.

Colin climbed up into the carriage.

"I will. You know I will."

"You can come back and visit," Leah called out as the carriage pulled away from the house.

Both Nathan and Leah ran alongside of it as it rolled down Main Street.

"Maybe we'll see each other again." Colin was crying unashamedly now. "Thank you, guys, for treatin' me square. You two were the best friends I ever had."

Unable to keep up with the wagon, Nathan and Leah stopped in the middle of the street. Colin turned around and stared at them. Then he shouted, "And don't forget when you write to me that it's Maddison with two *d*'s!" The words faded as the carriage disappeared in a cloud of dust and with the high-pitched squeak of wheels.

Nathan looked away from Leah and wiped his face and eyes on his bandanna.

Leah slipped her arm into Nathan's as they walked back toward Walker's Barber Shop. They didn't say anything until they sat down on the edge of the raised wooden sidewalk. Leah released her arm from Nathan's and rested her elbows on her knees, her chin in her hands.

"Well, the Lord sure does have surprises every day, don't He?" She sighed.

"It just doesn't seem real," Nathan added. "It all spins around in my head and makes everything confusing."

"Yeah, that's it." She nodded. "You jist keep hopin' that things is goin' to settle down quick, but they don't."

"I keep thinking about when it will be our turn."

"Yours and mine?"

"Yeah. Dad said we weren't movin' for a while since he

got hired on as a deputy sheriff, but if this town keeps goin' down, the day will come when we move."

"I suppose more folks will move with the bank gone."

"Yeah, they'll get awful tired ridin' into Battle Mountain Station to do their banking. What do you think, Leah—will your dad stay through the winter?"

"I don't know. Every day he reads them out-of-town papers more and more. And every day there seem to be fewer customers. Are you workin' tomorrow?"

"Yeah, I think so. I'll go check with Mr. Anderson in the morning . . . after I find Domingo and feed him."

"I told you he ain't there."

"Oh, he's probably back on his perch at the Heartford right now."

They looked at each other. Then Nathan bolted down the street toward the abandoned hotel.

"Nathan . . . wait! I cain't run fast in this dress . . . wait up!"

Suddenly Nathan slid to a stop and turned back toward her. "Well, hurry up!" he called.

They continued to the Heartford walking side by side.

"That's the first time you ever done that." She smiled.

"Did what?"

"Stopped and waited for me."

"Oh . . . well, it just seemed to be the right thing to do."

They rounded the corner by the closed Central Nevada Assay Office and hiked up to the hotel.

"See, I told you that old hawk was gone," Leah said triumphantly.

"Well, he might be over on the other . . ." Nathan trotted to the far side of the building with Leah right behind him.

"He's gone, Nathan. That's all there is to it."

"This is a good time to hunt. He'll be back later."

"I thought you said hawks like to hunt in the mornin's."

"Sure . . . normally . . . but I've not been around, and he's probably worried about—"

"Now don't you go tellin' me that hawk is worried about you!"

Nathan strained to gaze at the twilight sky. "No, he's probably worried about his next meal. I'll come feed him in the morning."

"And I say he should be off in the wilderness someplace."

"Sure . . . when he's a little more mature, he'll—"

"He'll what? You think he's going to fly down and shake your hand and promise to write. Come on, Nathan. Hawks don't say goodbye." Leah turned and started walking back toward Main Street. Nathan tagged along behind.

Lord, not two of them in one day. Domingo was just a bird, but he was part of my routine, part of daily life. I just don't want it all to fall apart at once. Please, Lord. I got to at least say goodbye to that hawk.

■

The next morning the topic of conversation on the sidewalks of Galena centered on just how long each person was planning on staying before they moved elsewhere.

Many held on to the hope that the Shiloh Mine would reopen by August. At the height of the gold mining activity, sale of mining stock had flowed without control. Although Nathan didn't really understand the details, right after Christmas the Shiloh's production fell off, the mining certificates drastically lost their value, and the principal owners were forced to sell out to a company in San Francisco. Company officials came to town and closed the mine, saying they would reopen soon under a new ownership.

But that was February. It was now July, and the only rumor they had from San Francisco was that the company who purchased major interest in the mine had sold it to some foreign investors. The only thing operating at the Shiloh were the huge steam-driven pumps that kept the lower tunnels from filling with water.

Meanwhile, many in Galena were waiting, hanging on to see what would happen to the mine. With the departure of its last bank, a good number in Galena, even those who still held some stock in the Shiloh, had decided it was time to move.

Even Mr. Anderson talked about closing the Mercantile.

"It's like kicking a man when he's down," he told Nathan the next morning. "You know, two years ago, if I got held up, I could recoup the losses in a couple of weeks. But now it will take all year if the money and firearms aren't recovered. That is, a whole year at the present rate of sales. If things slide more . . . well, I've moved and started a store before. I suppose I can do it again."

Nathan tossed his hat on a worn wooden peg by the back door of the store and pulled down his clerk's apron.

"Eh . . . Nate," Mr. Anderson continued, "what I'm leadin' to is this—I just can't afford to have you work here anymore, at least not for a while. Tony has a family to support, and now that your daddy's the deputy sheriff, you'll have groceries on the table . . . well, I hope you understand. You're a good worker, and I'll hire you any time I can afford it but . . ."

Nathan put the apron back on the hook.

"Yeah . . . sure. I, eh . . . I understand," he stammered, yanking his hat back on his head. "Just . . . eh, well, let me know if you'd like me to fill in for you or anything."

"Sorry, Nate," Mr. Anderson apologized. "I hope to have your pay by Saturday night. I don't have much cash right now, if you can wait 'til then."

"Huh? Oh, yeah. Sure. That's fine," Nathan mumbled as he slipped out the back door.

Scooting up the alley to Main Street, Nathan plodded along, head down, watching the cracks in the weathered wooden sidewalk.

Lord, it's gettin' worse. Every day things just keep falling apart. I don't understand. Why is this happening?

"Well, Mr. Nathan T. Riggins, you plannin' on marchin' right by me without speakin'?"

"Leah! Oh . . . hey, I'm sorry. I was just . . . thinkin'."

"Why ain't you at work?"

"I was laid off. Mr. Anderson can't afford to pay me anymore."

"No! Well . . . well," Leah stammered. "Did you feed that chicken hawk yet?"

"Eh . . . he wasn't there this morning. Maybe he is gone for good."

"Let's go for a picnic!" Leah beamed.

"What?"

"Saddle up Onepenny, and let's ride over to the Shoshones. I'll pack a dinner."

"I just lost my job and all you can think about is a picnic?"

"I cain't do nothin' about gettin' your job back, but I been wantin' a picnic all month. So why not today?"

"Well, I, eh . . . need to look for another job, and—"

"Do you want to go with me on a picnic or not?" Leah demanded.

A big smile broke across Nathan's face. "How come you can get me thinking about something else so quick?"

"'Cause of my absolutely irresistible beauty," she teased.

"Nope, that's not it," Nathan replied and dodged as Leah swung wildly to clobber him in the arm.

Within thirty minutes Leah, riding a gray mare that belonged to her father, and Nathan on Onepenny rode across the valley floor toward the Shoshone Mountains. When they crossed the river, Nathan turned back and glanced at the distant town of Galena in the western hills.

"They just come and go," he sighed.

"People or towns?" Leah questioned.

"Both . . . I guess. Maybe the luckiest people in the world are the ones that live in the same place all their lives. All their friends are always right there with them."

"And all their enemies," Leah added.

Nathan tuned back toward the Shoshones and spurred Onepenny to a trot. Leah bounced her way along trying to catch up.

"Well, I don't think it's so great to stay in one place your whole life," she hollered as she gained ground.

"Why not?"

"'Cause if you would have stayed in your home town, you'd still be in Indiana, and we would never have met."

"Did I ever mention this girl I knew back home? She would always say that one day we—"

"Don't you go tellin' me about some old Eastern girl, Nathan Riggins!"

"You brought it up," he insisted.

"I did not," she corrected. "I mentioned Indiana, but I didn't say nothin' about no girl! I'll race you to Rabbit Springs!"

"There's absolutely no way you can beat me," Nathan bragged.

In a haze of dust the two galloped up the gradual slope of the Shoshone Mountains.

Twenty minutes later, with Onepenny worked at full lather, Nathan pulled up near the springs and waited for Leah. She crashed into the clearing and ran the mare straight into the water of Rabbit Springs.

"I won!" she shouted.

"What do you mean, you won? I've been waiting for several minutes."

"Yes, but you were waiting ten feet from the springs. I got to the water first."

"That doesn't count!"

Leah stuck out her tongue and wrinkled her nose, causing the freckles across her face to wiggle. "It does too count, Nathan T. Riggins. You're just a poor loser."

Nathan slid off Onepenny and began to pull off his saddle.

"Is this where we're havin' the picnic?" Leah asked.

"No, let's leave the horses here. I know a place up at the top of the chaparral that will be great for a picnic."

"You been here before?"

"Yeah, I was just here two days ago—right before the robbery."

"How come you ain't never asked me to come out here before?"

Nathan ignored her question and hiked on up to the lookout rocks where he had spotted the pronghorns.

By the time Leah caught up with him, he was poking at a fire circle that smelled of a fairly recent campfire.

"I think someone was camping here last night," Nathan reported.

"Well, I don't blame them. Look how far you can see!" Leah pointed to the west. "Is that dark spot over on those distant mountains Galena?"

"Eh . . . yeah," Nathan muttered, "but what were they doin' camping here?"

"Well, it's a free country. They got just as much right as we do, don't they?"

"Yes, but this has always been my own private—"

"Nathan, you don't own this place."

"But . . . I wanted it to be my own private spot to come and think and plan and pray, you know?"

"You brought me up here," Leah pointed out.

"Sure, it can be for both of us. But now some strangers—it looks like they had several horses—have made it their camp too."

"They're just passin' through. I can't imagine why you're makin' such a big concern out of it. Shall I spread dinner right here?"

"Eh . . . yeah . . . sure. That's fine. But it doesn't make sense to me to camp up here. Down by the springs is the best place to put up for the night. You got a better view here, but it's not nearly as comfortable."

Nathan sat cross-legged and watched as Leah unrolled a small canvas tarp and began to pull fried chicken and biscuits out of a tin box.

After several minutes of talking about nothing but food, Nathan leaned back against a large boulder and stared out across the high mountain desert below them.

"Leah, do you think the Maddisons might return if we got their funds back?"

"We? You mean, you and me?"

"No, I mean if anyone was able to recover what was stolen from the bank, would they come back?"

"I don't know . . . once you say goodbye and all, it's kind of hard to return, don't you think? Besides, I don't think Colin's mama ever liked livin' here. Did you notice how she was always takin' trips and wantin' to go somewhere else?"

"Yeah . . . I suppose you're right. Anyway, I'm going to try to help Dad find the bank robbers. It's for certain they won't come back without the money."

"I thought your daddy didn't have a clue as to who they were."

"Well, perhaps I can dig around town and find out a little more. I don't know . . . I've got to do somethin', and since I'm not workin', it's a cinch I can't come up here for a picnic every day."

"I don't see why not," she teased. "Unless you don't like the company."

Nathan stared out across the desert and poked at the dead ashes in the rock fire ring with a short stick that had been burned on one end.

"I like the company. You're the only friend I've got left."

"That's why you tolerate me," she puffed. "I'm the only one left in town."

"Hey! Look at that!" Nathan pulled a short, light blue bottle out of the ashes. "They tossed something away."

"Nathan, that's one of them special Heartford Hotel liquor bottles. You know, the type they give when you stay in one of them big, old upstairs rooms."

"How do you know that?"

"'Cause Miss D'Imperio stayed there a little while, remember? 'Course she didn't drink none, but she did think the bottle was cute and had it sittin' right there on her dresser."

"But the Heartford has been closed for months. Where did they get this bottle?"

"They could have stayed there last fall and just emptied it yesterday."

"But it's only a little sample. Men who are camping out horseback wouldn't carry a sample of liquor around for months."

"What are you sayin', Nathan?"

"Well . . . maybe they took this from the Heartford recently."

"But it's closed."

"They could break in and steal stuff."

"Who would want to do that?"

"The same ones who robbed the bank and the Mercantile!" Nathan shouted.

Leah quickly looked around at the boulders. "You mean, we're sitting where them bank robbers spent the night?"

"Maybe. Let's go back and check out the Heartford. If we find out they stole things there, then maybe this is the trail."

"But," Leah questioned, "that was two days ago. They would have left a lot sooner than that."

"Uh . . . yeah, well . . . maybe they got lost or circled around. Yeah, that's it! Perhaps they went north to throw everyone off and then circled east! Let's go back to Galena."

"Right now?" she protested. "We ain't even finished the cake."

"We can eat it on the way home. Pack up the goods. I want to mark their trail with rocks, you know, just in case Dad wants to ride out here and look at this camp."

"Well, Nathan T. Riggins, you surely know how to show a girl a grand time."

"Huh?"

"Oh, nothin'!" Leah sighed in disgust.

5

Nathan wanted to ride right up to the Heartford Hotel and look around immediately.

But there were chores to do.

He rubbed down Onepenny and then Leah's mare. He grained them, checked their hooves, and put all the tack carefully in its place. Leah had hiked down the street from the livery to her house to put up the picnic supplies.

Then Nathan checked in with his mother.

"You're back early," she observed.

"Yeah . . . I, eh, we thought we might—," Nathan mumbled.

"You were nice to Leah, weren't you?"

"Huh? Oh . . . sure. I'm always nice to Leah. Say, where's Dad?"

"He said he heard that Big-Fist Tom might have seen some strangers pass his way a couple of days ago, so he rode out to visit with him."

"South of town? No, they didn't go south. They went . . ."

"You know something about this?" his mother asked.

"Well, actually, not yet . . . but maybe. We did find a new camp over in the Shoshones. It could have been the bank robbers."

"Or any of 1,000 other people in this county. Now don't you go meddlin' around and get into trouble."

"No, ma'am. I think I'll go down to the Heartford now."

"I don't want you too disappointed if that hawk's flown off. It was bound to happen."

"That's what Leah keeps telling me."

"Before you go, split some wood for the cookstove for supper."

"Yes, ma'am."

Ten minutes later Nathan came in carrying an arm load of split white pine. "Mother, did you notice that Tona's not even getting up anymore? He just lays there. He'll get all stove-up if he doesn't move around more."

"I'm afraid Tona's doing the best he can, Nathan. He's just . . . well, Nate . . ." His mother looked away. "Your father thinks Tona's dying."

"No! He's just having a bad spell. It's probably the heat. Come fall he'll be running around again," Nathan argued.

"I sure hope so. Are you leaving now?"

"Yeah, Leah and I thought we would—"

"Leah's going with you?" she asked.

"Eh . . . yeah. That's proper, isn't it?"

"You're spending a lot of time with that young lady this summer."

Nathan pulled on his hat and turned to the door. "But everyone else is moving away."

"Do you know what I hear from the ladies around town?" she asked.

"What?"

"They say, 'My, your Nathan and that Miss Walker certainly make a handsome pair.'"

Nathan could feel his face flush. "That's okay, isn't it?"

"Oh, it's quite acceptable when you're sixteen. But you're barely fourteen," she reminded him.

"So . . . you think I shouldn't . . . spend so much time with Leah?"

His mother took a deep breath and sighed. "Well, no, that's not it. I just . . . I want you to treat her proper. She's not merely some neighbor kid down the street. She's special, and if I ever hear of you being mean, well, your father and I will both take you out behind the woodpile."

"Yes, ma'am. I'll be home for supper." He left the house making sure to close the front door as quietly as possible.

Lord, I think Mom's kind of worried about everything lately. Help her to relax and trust You more about leading our family. And, Lord, I surely do want to treat Leah proper.

Nathan stepped into Walker's Barber Shop and noticed that Leah's father was busy with a customer.

"Excuse me, Mr. Walker, is Leah upstairs?"

"Yeah, but I, eh . . . don't think—"

"I'll go see her."

"Well, you might want to . . ." Mr. Walker hesitated.

"Thank you, sir." Nathan spun at the front door and ran back outside. He heard Mr. Walker say, "That's the lad I was tellin' you about."

Telling him what about me?

Nathan's boots tromped up the rough-cut wooden stairs on the outside of the barber shop to the house above. He knocked on the door. Leah's stepmother met him at the door.

"Oh, hi, Mrs. Walker. I was lookin' for Leah."

"Yes?"

"Well, is she here?"

"Yes, she is, Nathan."

"Oh . . . I mean, could I visit with her a minute? I wanted to . . . we were—"

"Nathan, Leah's not feelin' too well right now. Perhaps you could stop back later?"

"But we were going to—"

"I'm sorry, she's resting," Mrs. Walker added with finality.

"Yes, ma'am. Well, could you please tell her I stopped to see her? Tell her I'm headin' down to . . . feed Domingo."

"I'll tell her."

Nathan sauntered down the steps, pausing several times. *This doesn't make any sense. We just spent the morning together. She was feelin' fine. We laughed and raced. She promised to go with me to the Heartford. Did I miss something, Lord? What did I say?*

Hiking down the alley to the Heartford, Nathan reviewed the morning and remembered the little blue bottle in the ashes near Rabbit Springs.

"Well, I'm goin' to look around the hotel," he mumbled.

Not finding any trace of Domingo on the roof of the Heartford, Nathan circled the old building. The front door was boarded shut, as were all of the windows facing the front porch. Hiking up the hill and around to the back of the building, he noticed nothing unusual until he found a mint plant that had been struggling to grow on the shady side of the building just outside a kitchen window. The plant was withered and looked as if it had been stepped on recently.

Poking at the window, Nathan couldn't get it to swing out. He pulled out his folding knife and slipped a blade between the frame and the sill. The window swung out freely.

"That's how someone could get in." He pulled himself up to the window and climbed through. "Now, Lord, I don't normally crawl into someone else's building. But they say that the McBrineys just walked away and abandoned this hotel. I don't have any idea who to ask for permission."

The kitchen was dark and the air stale. He could see boot tracks in the dust across the wooden floor. "Man, he must be wearin' big spurs 'cause look how those rowels are draggin'."

He walked out into the dining area of the hotel and then to the parlor.

I didn't think they left all the furniture. Everything's still sitting right where it used to be. There's Mr. McBriney's desk. It seems funny not to see him there chewing on that cigar and sorting through those statements.

Well, I've never been upstairs, but Leah said that's where they gave away those little blue bottles.

At the top of the wide, dust-caked mahogany staircase, Nathan discovered a long hall and sixteen doors, each door looking as if it led to a hotel room.

One at a time he entered the rooms. Most were the same. A bed with linen folded and stacked at the foot, a dresser with an empty wash basin, a small wardrobe closet, and padded seat chair. Some of the rooms had several pictures and mirrors. Others had none at all. All the rooms had a liquor sample in a blue bottle sitting by the wash basin.

Nathan was working his way east down the hall when he thought he heard a noise in the next room. Scurrying into the room at the southeast corner of the two-story hotel, Nathan was shocked at the sight.

"Domingo! But what . . ."

The hawk was walking across the floor toward Nathan.

Then it turned and scooted behind the bed. Glancing around, Nathan noticed that there were feathers and bird droppings scattered around the room.

"You've been in here for two days! How'd you get in here? You sure didn't open the kitchen window with your pocket knife, did you?"

Nathan reached to the back of his trousers and pulled out the heavy leather glove with the long, fringed gauntlet. Then he whistled at the bird.

"Come on, boy. I'll get you out of here. Come on, Domingo, come on!"

The bird hopped out from behind the bed, walked toward Nathan, lifted his wings about halfway, and then put them down without flapping them.

"You about worn out? You must be starved . . . and thirsty. There's no water in here!"

Nathan got down on his hands and knees and laid the gloved arm in front of the bird. Domingo took a couple of steps and hopped onto the glove.

"Okay. Now you just hang on, and I'll get you outside."

Nathan scooted out of the room with Domingo teetering on his arm. Gliding down the stairs as smoothly as possible, he pushed his way into the kitchen, hustled past the chopping block, and threw open the window.

"All right, boy, you fly out there to someplace safe, and I'll find you something to . . ."

The big hawk spread his wings and glided to the ground, but did not try to fly.

"Are you hurt? Hungry? You're starving to death, aren't you?"

Nathan crawled back out of the hotel and bent low to the ground, allowing Domingo to hop back on his arm.

"Well, I can't leave you on the ground 'cause the dogs would get you, and you can't fly, so . . ." Scouting around, Nathan ran up the hill behind the hotel to the privies. Lifting the bird high, he jiggled his arm, signaling the bird to jump off.

"You stay up there on the outhouse roof. I'll get you some water and food. You wait for me, you understand?"

Nathan ran all the way home. Finding his mother gone, he filled a tin cup with water from the pump and grabbed a cooked pork chop lying under a towel next to the sink.

Arriving back at the Heartford, Nathan was relieved to find Domingo standing exactly where he had left him. He propped the water cup on top of the roof, and the brown and white hawk hopped over for a drink. Taking out his knife, Nathan sliced small bites off the pork chop and sprinkled them across the shake roof of the outhouse.

Domingo quickly swallowed several of the portions, took another drink, and then hopped up to the top ridge of the out-house.

"You going to be all right now? What were you doing in there anyway? Somebody had a window open. That's it. There had to be someone in the hotel to open a window! I sure wish you could talk. On second thought, you'd just bawl me out for leavin' you in there for two days."

Nathan shoved his penknife back into his pocket and tramped down to the hotel, once again climbing in through the kitchen window. Leaping the stairs two at a time, he returned to the room on the southeast corner. Other than Domingo's droppings, Nathan couldn't find anything unusual about the room.

Even that little blue bottle is still by the basin. Maybe Domingo found a hole in the ceiling and—

"Look at that!" he blurted out. "You can see the front of the bank from here. A guy could sit here and see just who was coming in and going out. And the back door of the Mercantile!

"You could signal others when to go in and even which way to ride out of town. 'Course, you'd have to open the window to signal. Someone could sit up here and direct both holdups."

Leaving the corner room, Nathan swung open the door of the room directly across the hall. It was the one room he had not checked out earlier.

"Hey . . . this is it! Someone's been staying in this room!"

He smelled cigarette smoke. In the corner were assorted empty air-tight fruit tins. Stale bread littered the floor, and there was an empty whiskey bottle lying on top of the mattress. Nathan pulled out the drawers of the dresser and found a heavy cotton sack with "Dr. Barker's Horse Liniment" printed on the front, under which was hand-written ".44-40."

"That's the Mercantile's loose bullet bag! The ones that robbed the store were up here!"

Nathan hustled down the stairs carrying the empty sack. Climbing out the kitchen window, he carefully closed it and ran up the alley toward his house.

"Domingo, when you feel strong, you better get back on the roof of the Heartford," he yelled as he glanced back at the privy.

His mother was sitting on the front porch doing needlework when he huffed his way into the yard. Tona lifted his head and beat his tail on the porch.

"What's the matter?" his mother asked.

67

"Is Daddy home yet?"

"Not yet. Why?"

"I found some evidence from the outlaws."

"What kind of evidence?"

"The cotton sack Mr. Anderson used for the loose .44-40 bullets at the Mercantile. It was stolen along with some revolvers."

"Where did you find it?"

"Upstairs in one of the rooms of the Heartford Hotel."

"Nathan Riggins, what were you doing up there? That hotel is private property. I mean, someone somewhere owns it. I think."

"I was letting Domingo out. He got caught in one of the rooms, and I brought him out. But I found this up there."

"I'm sure your father will be very interested in it. But he won't be home for a couple more hours."

"A couple hours! Maybe I'll ride out to Big-Fist Tom's."

"You'd better go see Leah first."

"Leah? I went over there, and she was sick or something. Her stepmother said she couldn't visit."

"Well, she was over here a short while ago and quite upset, I might add. What did you do or say?"

"Me? I didn't do anything! We had a great time, and then she turns up sick."

"Well, stop by and see her on the way out to Big-Fist Tom's."

"Yes, ma'am, I will."

Tona looked up at Nathan and let out a faint, high-pitched bark.

"Nathan, I think he wants to go with you."

"Mom . . . I'll have to carry him the whole way."

"Well, whatever. But it seems like Tona's earned a free ride over the years that he's watched over you."

Nathan looked down at the dog whose only hint of happiness was the slapping of his tail on the porch.

"Yeah, you're right. He can have a ride any time. Wait here, boy, and I'll go saddle up Onepenny."

"Why don't you take your carbine," his mother urged. "You might see a varmit along the way, and Tona would enjoy the hunt."

"Eh . . . yeah, I'll take it."

As he saddled Onepenny, he wondered why his mother was suddenly so concerned about Tona's happiness. At her insistence, he tied his jacket on behind the cantle, lashed the scabbard and carbine to the left side of the saddle, and hoisted Tona into place.

"Did you get your canteen?"

"Yes, ma'am, it's in my saddlebags. But I'm just going to Big-Fist Tom's."

"Well, Tona might get thirsty. He hasn't felt too good today. I stuck some biscuits in the pocket of your jacket."

"Tona doesn't eat biscuits."

"Those are for you and your father. He probably skipped dinner. And don't forget to stop by and see Leah."

"Yes, ma'am."

Nathan rode up to Walker's Barber Shop. Carefully setting Tona on Onepenny's rump, he climbed down out of the saddle.

"Now you two wait for me . . . understand?"

Nathan left the reins dropped to the dirt road. Onepenny stood motionless, and Tona laid his head on Nathan's jacket and closed his eyes.

He had just started up the outside stairs when Mr. Walker called to him from inside the barber shop.

"Nathan?"

"Yes, sir?" He spun on the step and ducked into the barber shop. Nathan noticed that the man who had earlier been getting a haircut now sat on a bench inside the shop. There were business papers spread across a little table.

"Nathan, are you still lookin' for Leah?"

"Yes, sir. Mama said she stopped by after I was here. Is she feelin' any better?"

"I don't think so. That's what I want to talk to you about."

"Mr. Walker, I can't think of one thing I did or said that would upset Leah. I promise you, I've always treated her square."

"No, no." Mr. Walker smiled. "She's not upset because of you. You've been the best influence she's ever had in her life. From the time you bought her those black shoes to the way you helped her know about God. In fact, I guess you two have got along too well."

"What do you mean," Nathan asked. "What's troubling her?"

"Well, I promised to let Leah tell you, but I'm worried sick about her. So don't let on that you know anything. You see, this is Mr. Hiram Silverman from Salt Lake City, and he just bought my barber shop."

"What? You sold out?"

"Yep. I figured it was time."

"But . . . what are you goin' to do? You aren't going to move, are you?"

"Yes, we'll be moving by the end of the month."

"But where?" Nathan moaned.

"We'll take a look at Austin and White Pine County. Maybe we'll try Arizona. Just not sure, Nate."

"But . . . but Leah can't move! I'll . . . sorely miss her!" Nathan gulped. "This just about breaks my heart."

"Well, there's a young lady who feels the exact same way, I assure you."

"Can I go up and see her?"

"Now it's not that easy. She's not home."

"Where is she? I've got to see her!"

"That's the problem. When she couldn't find you at home, she said she was goin' to saddle the mare and ride to where she could think and plan and pray. When I asked her where that was, she said it was a secret place, but you would know."

"Over by Rabbit Springs! We were just out there this morning."

"I'm surely glad you know where it is. Would you have time to ride out there and make sure she's all right?" Mr. Walker asked.

"Yes, sir, I've got Onepenny, and I'll . . . . Dad! Listen, Mr. Walker, I was on my way out to see if I could find my dad. He is out toward Big-Fist Tom's place. I think I found some evidence that will help catch the bank robbers."

"Oh . . . well, maybe you should go ahead and—"

"No, sir. Leah's more important than all the bank robbers on earth. If you see my dad come through town, tell him I found out that the outlaws holed up in the old Heartford Hotel before and after the crime. I think they camped near Rabbit Springs, which means they're probably in Utah by now."

Nathan turned toward the door. "And . . . eh, would you tell him where I went?"

"I'll tell him, Nate. And thanks for going after Leah."

"Mr. Walker, I've never met anyone I like bein' with more than Leah—you know, other than my mama and daddy."

Nathan wanted to race off toward the Shoshone Mountains, but instead he set a pace that he knew Onepenny could keep up. Tona rode in his lap. The hot breeze dried his face even as the sun started its gradual summer descent. When he crossed the river, he pushed his hat back and let it hang by the stampede string on his back.

Lord, this is like a horrible, horrible nightmare. It's like everything and everyone important to me is being taken away. It's not fair! I don't want to . . . I can't imagine . . . Lord, do You know what it's like when all your friends just take off at once?

After a long pause, Nathan glanced up at the blue sky.

Yeah, You know, don't You? They all ran away and left You there on the cross. And You went ahead and did what needed to be done. Well, You're goin' to have to get me through 'cause in my heart I feel like I'm dyin'.

As he expected, Leah had hobbled the gray mare near Rabbit Springs. Nathan loosened the cinch on Onepenny but left him saddled. He took Tona to the spring to give him a drink and then placed him in the shade.

Pulling his Winchester .44-40 carbine from the scabbard, he hiked up the hill to the rock-pile lookout.

At a distance he spotted Leah waiting for him.

When he got closer, he could tell she had been crying.

"He told you, didn't he?" she called as he approached.

"Your daddy?"

72

"Yeah, I asked him to let me tell you."

"He told me. Leah, he was worried sick about you and didn't know where you had ridden off to."

"Well, it's okay 'cause I couldn't figure out what to say to you. It's all I can do to even mention it now."

"I know. When he told me, I felt like . . . like—"

"Like you been robbed?" she asked.

"Yeah . . . that's it." Nathan sat down on the rocks next to Leah. "It's crazy. It's like someone picked up the whole world and is shakin' it out. Everything that used to be here is fallin' over there. Nothing's the same. Everything's different."

"I ain't movin', Nathan."

"What?"

"I done made up my mind I ain't movin'!" she insisted.

"But your daddy said that—"

"If he makes me move, I'll jist run away from home and come back to Galena."

"But what would you do? Where would you live?" Nathan asked.

"I'll get me a job at the Drover's Cafe and rent a room of my own. Maybe your mama would rent me that back room at your house. Do you think she'd rent it to me?"

The tears streamed down her face.

"Leah, I don't think either one of us believes that story."

"Well, it ain't fair. Nathan, I been prayin' and prayin' and prayin' that you and me wouldn't have to move. I didn't ask for money or jewelry or to be famous or to be beautiful. All I ever wanted was for you and me to have a chance to grow up in the same town. Nathan, that wouldn't cost God nothin'. Why won't God answer my prayer?"

Nathan stared for a long time across the high desert floor beneath them.

"I don't know, Leah. One time, two years ago, when I was lost out in these mountains and couldn't find my parents, I thought God had forgotten me completely. But when it was all over, I looked back and realized that God was with me all the time. Maybe it's the same now."

"Yeah, well, if God's doin' it," she asked sniffing, "how come it hurts so bad?"

6

Leah stood up on top of the boulder and stared out at the valley floor. "Nathan, how many times have you ever moved?"

"Eh, just once. You know, from our farm in Indiana."

"That's it? You only lived in two places?"

"Yeah. How about you, Leah? How many houses have you lived in?"

"Twenty-three. But I wouldn't call all of 'em houses. We lived in a tent here in Galena before the barber shop was built."

"How come your daddy moves so often?"

Leah jumped off the boulder and stumbled toward Nathan. He reached out and caught her. Then she pulled back and brushed off her blue dress. "He says it's his Indian blood."

"Indian blood?"

"My grandma was half-Indian, you know."

"I didn't know that. How come you never told me that?" Nathan asked.

"'Cause most kids make fun of me when I tell 'em. Besides, there are other things you don't know about me, Nathan T. Riggins." Then she broke into a wide smile. "'Course, there ain't many things you don't know."

"Your father said maybe you'd move to Austin," Nathan

added. "With my daddy being a sheriff's deputy now, we might have to move to Austin someday."

"Yeah, he also said we might move to Tombstone. Talk about a dumb name for a town! You know, when I was little, I liked movin'," Leah continued. "Every new place was a new adventure. There was new streets to explore, new kids to play with, and always the hope that things would be better than the last place. Well, Galena is the place where they all got better." Leah's eyes teared up again. "What are we goin' to do, Nathan?"

"I, eh, I think," Nathan stammered, "well, I think we ought to just pretend that nothing's different. Maybe you will move in two weeks . . . maybe you won't. Maybe *I'll* be the one to move first. Who knows? In the meantime, we ought to go ahead and do what we would be doin' if you weren't moving. Maybe it's our last two weeks of living in the same town, but they ought to be fun weeks and not sad ones. Right?"

"Yeah, I like that." Leah reached down and snapped off a tiny red flower growing on a leafless plant that hugged tight to the mountainside. "What would we be doin'?"

"I think we ought to search for the trail of those outlaws who camped up here."

"How do you know it was outlaws?"

"Because of the dragging Spanish rowel. The same track was in the dust at the Heartford where I found the bullet bag."

"The what? The Heartford? Were you in the Heartford?"

"Yeah, listen, I'll tell you all about it while we look for some tracks," Nathan suggested.

Nathan explained his discoveries in the Heartford Hotel as they hiked over the crest of the hill.

"Are we goin' to track 'em down then?" Leah asked.

"I don't want to . . . you know, catch up with them," Nathan admitted. "But it wouldn't hurt to mark their trail for a while before the wind blows it away. Let's get the horses."

Within minutes they were following the hoofprints of five men who had ridden east from the campfire. Nathan leaned over his saddle horn, searching for prints on the rocky desert hillside. Tona curled up in Leah's lap as she rode the gray mare.

"Tona don't look so good, does he?" Leah asked.

Nathan sat up straight in the saddle. "Maybe I should have left him out there with the Rialtos. Then I wouldn't have to watch him go down."

"I like Tona," Leah commented.

"Well, the feeling's mutual. You know how he doesn't want anyone to touch him but me and you."

"And them Rialto girls."

"Yeah, them too."

"Maybe when I run away, I could go live with them," Leah said pondering.

"You can't run away."

"How come?"

"'Cause the Lord would hound you to go back home, and you know it," Nathan insisted. "Hey . . . look at this!"

"I don't see nothin'."

"The tracks split. Can't you see it?"

"What do you mean, they split?"

"Well, two horses turned straight east."

"Over them mountains?"

"I guess."

"How about the other three?"

"They're pointing south."

"There ain't nothin' south of here, is there?" Leah asked.

"Not that I know of . . . until you get to Pony Canyon and Austin."

"Well, what are we goin' to do now?"

"I think we ought to mark both trails and go home. It's late, and I ought to tell my dad what's happening."

"Can I eat supper at your house?"

"Eh . . . sure, I mean, I'll have to ask my mother, but she's never turned anyone down for a meal. How come you want to eat at our house?"

"'Cause all they'll be talkin' about at my house is movin', and I don't aim to sit around all evenin' with that on my mind."

Neither said anything for several minutes as Nathan slipped off Onepenny and piled rock markers in the directions of both sets of riders.

They turned the horses west and began the descent back to the valley floor.

"Colin was lucky," Leah blurted out.

"Lucky?"

"Yeah, they just up and moved. He didn't have to think about it very long. Maybe that's the way to do it. Maybe I should tell Daddy that we should just up and move tomorrow."

"Tomorrow? No!" Nathan exploded.

"How come? You're the one that gets to stay in Galena," she reminded him.

"Yeah, but Galena won't be the same without you. You were just about the first one I talked to and . . . ."

"And what, Nathan T. Riggins?"

"Well, you know . . . we had some good times . . . and I'll really miss you," he blurted out.

Again they rode in silence.

Stopping at the little creek, they let the horses drink. Nathan poured a handful of water from his canteen and let Tona lap it up. Then he took a deep breath and filled his lungs with the pungent smell of sage.

"What you been thinkin' about?" she asked him.

"About that time you slipped off the back of Onepenny and fell in the mud." Nathan laughed.

"Oh, that's real nice. I'm all sad about movin', and you're pokin' fun at me."

"You know what I like about you?" he probed.

"What?"

"Nothing's ever boring when we're together." Nathan pulled off his bandanna and wiped the dirt out of the corners of his eyes.

"You know what I been thinkin' about?" she asked.

"No, what?"

"Writin' letters. I ain't too good at it. You won't shame me if I spell them words all wrong, will you? I am gettin' better, you know."

"I promise I won't be critical. But I don't want to talk about you movin'."

"Well, whether we talk about it or not, it's goin' to happen."

"I'm prayin' you'll stay."

"That would take a miracle." She shrugged.

"The Lord's pretty good at miracles," Nathan reminded her as he spurred Onepenny across the creekbed.

■

Some of the lanterns were already lit when they made their way back into Galena. After returning Tona to the braided rug on the porch, Nathan put the horses away and walked Leah back to her house. He waited at the bottom of the outside stairs next to the barber shop.

Bounding down the stairs, Leah was all smiles. "I kin have supper with you! Guess what?"

"You're not moving?"

She wrinkled her freckle-covered nose. "No, but it is sort of good news. Daddy and Mr. Silverman are goin' to Austin to file some papers. My stepmother is goin' with them."

"Are you going, too?"

"Nope." She grinned. "They said I didn't have to go."

"They're goin' to let you stay here by yourself?"

Leah dropped her smile and frowned.

"No, they ain't goin' to let me stay by myself. I'm goin' to stay at your house."

"My house? Really? Did you ask my mother already?"

"Nope, but she'll agree to let me stay, won't she? It's just for a few days."

"Well . . . I, eh . . . sure, I reckon she will."

■

She did.

That evening Nathan told his father the whole story about finding the bullet bag in the Heartford and the tracks near Rabbit Springs. Nathan and Leah made plans to ride out the next morning with Mr. Riggins and see if they could find the trail.

Leah helped Mrs. Riggins with the dishes. Then all four

of them retired to the coolness of the front porch. His mother started to sing "Shenandoah," and soon the others joined in. For the next two hours they talked, sang, laughed, and teased. Mr. Riggins finally signaled that it was time to turn in for the night.

Leah and Nathan stayed on the porch for a few minutes after his parents re-entered the house.

"You know why I like comin' over to your house?" she asked him.

"How come?"

"'Cause everybody likes everybody, and there ain't no drinkin', and there ain't ever no yellin' or nothin'."

"Well, we don't . . . have that much fun all the time. I mean, sometimes it's pretty boring," Nathan admitted. "Too bad you weren't my sister. Think of all—"

"That's dumb," Leah interrupted. "I don't want to be your sister!"

"No, no, what I meant was that—"

"Nathan T. Riggins, I cain't understand how come you are so smart in school and so dumb about other things!"

■

Later that night Nathan lay in his own bed and stared out the window at the star-filled night.

Lord, how come I always say things that make Leah mad? And . . . You know . . . if You wanted to change her daddy's mind about movin', well, I would really like that.

Nathan fell asleep and dreamed that he was walking down Main Street in Galena, but it was totally empty. Everyone, including his parents, had moved away, and he couldn't even find his house. The next morning he woke up with his nightshirt wet with sweat.

Nathan dressed and scooted outside to gather an arm load of wood for the cookstove. He noticed that Tona was breathing heavily, but the dog didn't wake up as he walked by. The morning air felt dry and stale. The mountains to the east could barely be seen through the dusty haze.

"Mother, I think that trip yesterday wore Tona out. Maybe I better not take him anymore."

"Perhaps you're right. Nathan, your father went to Austin this morning," she announced.

"He what?"

"A telegram came in early stating that the sheriff had been shot in a gunfight with some bank robbers. They need him in Austin."

"But we were . . . I mean . . . the sheriff's shot? Is he dead?"

"The telegram only said he was shot. Your father thinks it might be the same men who robbed the bank up here. But he did have a job for you."

"What's that?"

"Well, you said the trail looked like three men went south from Rabbit Springs?"

"Yeah, and the other two went east."

"Yes, he wants you to ride out and follow the two east just to Coyote Creek. He wants to know if they kept going east after the creek or if they turned some other direction."

"He wants me to do that?"

"Yes, he said you're the best tracker he has, but he doesn't want you following them any further than the creek."

"Yes, ma'am. Eh . . . Leah can go with me, can't she?"

"That's why I'm packing you two a lunch," his mother answered.

"I've got to go check on the horses and feed Domingo."

"I thought you fed that hawk yesterday."

"I did, but after not eating in a while, I figured he might need a little extra."

■

In the livery Nathan pulled down some hay for the horses in the corral and pumped up a little more water for the trough.

Lord, keep Dad safe. I think Mother gets more worried every time he goes out. Help her to relax, too.

Main Street was almost deserted as he hiked up the hill toward the Heartford Hotel. Someone across town was banging a hammer, and the sound drifted up the street. A lone horse tied in front of the Drover's Cafe swished its tail, providing the only movement in sight.

He scanned the roof line of the hotel.

"Okay, Domingo, where did you go? Did you stay on the privy all night?"

Running to the back of the hotel, he searched everywhere for the hawk.

Well, I don't see any feathers, so I guess nothing ate him. Maybe he just flew off for a hunt. I thought he'd probably be hungry. One more pass around the hotel revealed no clues as to the hawk's location. Nathan trudged up the alley to his house.

■

He didn't say much on the ride back out to Rabbit Springs. Mainly he listened to Leah, who seemed to be in a hurry to shove three years of conversation into one morning.

"See, I reckon to have a house with fruit trees out back and a shade tree in the front large enough to have a push swing. You know the kind I mean? Like some folks have on their porch, but I want one out in the yard. Those on-the-porch ones don't swing very high, and I figure why have a swing if it don't swing high? You like to swing, don't you?

"I knew a girl once—her name was Priscilla P. Preston . . . no, really, that was her name. Well, she got sick every time we got in a swing. I mean, she'd lose her lunch right there on the porch. I ain't never knowed anyone else who got sick in a swing, did you? Well, I don't guess anything like that makes me sick. I got sick one time on top of a barn. Did I ever tell you about when I was stuck on top of a barn all night long?"

Nathan started to speak.

"I didn't think so," she barged on. "See, I was going to run away from home when I was about six, but there weren't no place to go. So I decided to hide in the barn and pretend like I run away. But then I got scared that Daddy would find me in the hayloft, so I crawled up on the roof of the barn. You know, it had one of them cupolas up on top, so I hid up there.

"Well, I heard them a callin' and callin', but I wasn't about to let on where I was. But when it started to get dark, I realized that I couldn't get down. When I started easing down the roof, I turned and looked at the ground. I got so scared I threw up all over the roof."

"You were up there all night?" Nathan asked.

"Not exactly all night. My daddy came out after dark

and started yellin' for me again. That's when I hollered at him that I was on the roof."

"What did he do?"

"He got me off the roof, washed me up, whipped my behind, gave me a hug and a kiss, and then tucked me in bed."

"Did he swat you hard?"

"I don't remember." Leah shrugged. "But he kissed me tender. I remember that. I think he was more scared than mad."

Leah continued the nonstop conversation all the way to Rabbit Springs and beyond. When they came to the marker where the outlaws' trail divided, Nathan slid down off Onepenny and examined the tracks.

"How come you ain't been talkin' much?" Leah asked. "What you been thinkin' about?"

"Oh, I've been listening to you . . . and thinking about . . . well, if those three that robbed the bank in Austin are part of this gang, maybe they'll ride back up here to follow these two."

"You mean there might be bank robbers on the trail?" she asked.

"Yeah. Maybe the kind that shoot sheriffs."

"They wouldn't ride back up here, would they?" Leah asked.

"*¿Quién sabe?*" Nathan shrugged.

He climbed back on Onepenny, and they followed the tracks of the two riders east until they came to Coyote Creek, which was no more than three feet wide.

"Which way did they go?"

"It looks like they went north." Nathan motioned. "They weren't worried about being followed. Look at all the tracks they left."

"Where would they go to the north?"

"Maybe Elko . . . maybe to catch the train—"

"Or rob it!" Leah suggested. "Are we going back now?"

"It's about noon. Let's rest the horses and eat. Then we can head back," Nathan recommended.

"What if them robbers are still out here?" she asked.

"If you were an outlaw, would you camp right out here in the open?"

"Eh . . . no, I don't guess I would. I'll spread out dinner. Your mama sure is a good cook, Nathan. Do you think she'd teach me how to cook? I got two weeks before we move. I think I could learn a lot in two weeks. Did your mama ever teach anyone to cook? I heard of a boy once whose mama taught him. I don't think a boy ought to cook. 'Course, I don't mean around a chuck wagon. That's different and . . ."

Nathan was still listening to Leah when he finished eating and began packing the supplies back on Onepenny.

"Hey," he shouted, "did you see that?" He waved wildly to the north.

"What?" Leah jumped to her feet and stared.

"Pronghorns! I think I saw some over toward those hills!"

"You saw antelope? I don't see nothin'."

"They're up there, I tell you. Can't you see them? A dark brown spot two-thirds of the way up the mountain. Come on, let's go hunting."

"Hunting? I don't want to go—"

"Come on, Leah. I've been wanting to get one for months."

"I ain't goin' to shoot none, but I'll watch you. Me and

that old mare cain't keep up with you two. So go on, and we'll catch up. But don't you go leavin' us stranded."

"See those trees up on that distant hill?" Nathan pointed.

"I don't see no trees."

"That dark green color on the side of that range? See it? That's some kind of trees. I'll meet you there. Can you finish cleaning up?"

"Oh, sure, eat and run. That's the way you boys are, never takin' time to listen to what a girl has to say," she teased.

"I've been listening all morning long," Nathan reminded her.

"But I ain't got to the important part yet," she protested. "Go on. Go hunt your antelope."

"I'll see you at the trees," Nathan shouted as he swung up into the saddle and pulled his carbine from the scabbard.

"Oh, I'll meet you in them trees, providin' I don't get a better offer," she pouted.

Nathan whipped around and looked back at Leah.

She stuck out her tongue.

For some reason he couldn't explain, he stuck out his tongue in return.

Within seconds he was galloping north.

Pulling up at the bottom of a draw, Nathan checked on the wind, felt it blowing in from the northwest, and then rode east.

No reason for them to catch my scent before I get a little closer.

On an incline to the east he looked back and could see the animals grazing on a small dry meadow near the juniper grove.

"Okay, boy, you wait here." Nathan slipped down from the saddle and let Onepenny's reins drop.

He cocked the lever on his Winchester carbine and slowly stalked around the hillside, approaching the short juniper trees.

If I can make it to the trees, I'll sneak right up to the edge and pick out a good-sized one!

Crouching behind the first few trees, he kept his eyes focused straight ahead. He stepped slowly, lightly, and then lifted the carbine to his shoulder. He could feel the plate on the stock press tight against his right shoulder; the trigger felt cool to his finger; the gun felt light . . . one more tree and Nathan would come within view of the prey. They would see him, too, but he knew he would be close enough to get off a good shot. Nathan held his breath and . . .

"Drop the gun, kid, or you'll never live to see your mama!"

The man with the rough voice jammed a Colt .44 into Nathan's ribs.

7

The hairs on the back of Nathan's neck bristled; a heaviness hit the pit of his stomach, and a lump welled up in his throat. He let the hammer down slowly on the carbine and then bent over and laid the gun in the dirt. Turning, he found himself staring at a thin man, almost six feet tall, holding a cocked revolver against Nathan's side. The man's wide-brimmed hat was pulled low, covering dark eyes. His face was unshaven, and his cheek bulged with tobacco.

"Who . . . who are you?" Nathan choked out.

"Don't matter none who I am. What matters is who you are and why you are sneaking up on our camp with a cocked gun."

"You . . . you . . . your camp?" Nathan stammered. "I, eh, I didn't see any camp. I was just hunting those antelope over there."

"Do those look like antelope?" the man growled. "There ain't nothin' over there but our horses."

"I can see that now . . . but from a distance . . . I thought I was . . . I mean, I'm sure I saw some pronghorns."

"Kid, you're wasting my time. I want to know what you was after!"

"I was huntin'. Honest!"

"Well, you found more than you bargained for, I can tell you that."

The man reached down and scooped up Nathan's carbine and shoved him back up the hill toward a thick clump of junipers.

"Where are you takin' me?" he protested.

"As if you didn't know." The man shoved the barrel of the revolver hard into Nathan's back. A sharp pain racked his ribs, and he stumbled forward.

"J. T., I'm bringin' in a snoopin' kid!" his captor hollered out as they came close to a fire circle and crude camp in a small clearing back in the junipers.

A hatless man in a dirty brown vest stepped out from behind a short tree. A shotgun rested across his left arm, and Nathan could see that the thumb and index finger of his right hand were missing.

"What's he doin' out here?" the man asked.

"Says he was huntin' antelope."

"Antelope? Now ain't that a coincidence. Here we are huntin' antelope, too. But we ain't had much luck, boy. Ain't nothin' around here close. Sit down . . . you want some coffee?"

"Eh . . . no." Nathan sat next to a fire circle that had long before been extinguished. "I thought there were some antelope just outside your camp, but I didn't know you were here."

"I say he's been spying on us, trying to steal our horses. Maybe we should just plug him," the first man suggested.

Ignoring that comment, the one with fingers missing asked, "Where you from, boy?"

"Eh . . . Galena. I live in Galena."

"Galena? Don't reckon I've ever heard of that one." The man looked Nathan straight in the eyes. "Is that near here?"

"Oh, it's over there to the west about . . . well, it's not all that far," he finished. "I'm really sorry for bustin' into your camp. I'll just be on my way now, and I promise I won't come over here again."

"You ain't goin' nowhere, boy. You see, we're the kind of fellas that like our privacy. Now you go traipsing back into Galena and telling everyone about the . . . eh, antelope hunters you seen out here, and, well, every Sunday hunter in the county will come ridin' this way poppin' off their repeatin' rifles. So we'll jist sit you here a spell."

"You got to let me go home!"

"I don't got to do nothin'! You understand that?" the man barked back.

Nathan heard the horses whinny on the other side of the junipers and turned to look. He counted at least a half-dozen unsaddled mounts.

"Go check on them horses. They ain't settled into that rope corral yet," the one called J. T. commanded.

"What you goin' to do with him?"

"Tie him to a tree and wait for Clayton and the others, I suppose."

Others? How many others?

After the first man went up the hill, the other turned to Nathan. "Where'd you tie your horse, boy? Now don't go tellin' me you walked all the way over here from Galena."

"Town's not all that far," Nathan tried to explain.

"I know how . . . anyway . . . where's your horse tied?"

"I, eh . . . didn't tie him. I was . . . I thought I was chasing antelope, and I left him over by the south edge of the trees. I don't know if he's still there."

"Well, now, that surely ain't very smart."

"I was huntin' antelope."

"And I say you was tryin' to steal our horses. Say, you ain't part Indian, are ya?"

The other man came back into the clearing.

"Brushy, you hike over and see if this boy's pony is on the south edge of the junipers like he said."

"He doesn't warm up quick to strangers," Nathan warned.

"If the cayuse gives ya any trouble, jist shoot it," J. T. called out.

"No! You can't do that!"

"You don't seem to understand, boy. You come sneakin' around camp, flashin' a cocked weapon, and tryin' to steal horses—I kin do anything I want. That's the rules."

"What rules?" Nathan protested.

"The rules of who holds the gun."

"J. T.," Brushy called out as he returned to the clearing, "I cain't find no horse out there."

"I told you, I didn't tie him up."

"Well, that's no matter. We got plenty of horses anyway."

"It looks like some riders coming up from the south . . . or maybe a dust devil blowin' out there," Brushy reported.

From the south? It's Leah . . . Lord, don't let her come up here! Keep her safe.

"Tie him up, and I'll go check on who's comin' in," the man with the missing fingers commanded.

Brushy shoved Nathan back against a short juniper. The

boy sat down and felt his arms jerked around behind his back and tied to the trunk of the tree.

Lord, if these are the bank robbers, then they don't mind shooting sheriffs . . . I want to get out of here. I want to get out real bad!

"Hey, Brushy! I think it's Clayton and the others. They're settin' a pretty good pace."

"Anybody followin' them?"

"Nope."

"That's a good sign." Brushy walked over to the edge of the clearing and stared south. "You suppose they pulled it off?"

"Yep. Ain't nothin' will stop Clayton but a bullet."

"How much you suppose they got?"

J. T. looked back at Nathan and then whispered a few words to Brushy. Then both men laughed and glanced back at him.

The others are coming in from Austin! They're killers! Don't let them find Leah!

Nathan tugged at the rope that secured him to the tree, straining to see who was approaching. He watched the column of dust come closer until all three men rode into the clump of junipers. He tried to hear the conversation, but he could only make out shouts, boasts, and laughter. He thought he heard one of them mention the word *sheriff,* which was followed by a curse and then some more laughter.

Finally all five men walked into the clearing.

"So this is the hombre who was tryin' to steal our horses?"

"I wasn't tryin' to steal your—"

"Boy, didn't your mama teach you not to lie?" he gruffed.

"But I—"

"Shut up, kid! Now, boys, pull your saddles and slap 'em on some fresh mounts. I don't figure to stay in this country any longer. Grab yourself some grub 'cause we got a long ride."

Nathan searched around for some way to escape. Every time he yanked on the ropes, they seemed to pinch tighter on his wrists.

If I could get free, I could dive for my carbine over next to the fire circle. Then I could . . . then I could get myself shot! Maybe this is a bad dream, Lord. Like the other night when I thought everyone had left Galena. This would be a real good time to wake up in my bed and—

"You did a good job of gettin' horses, J. T.," he heard Clayton call out. "They look fast enough to run all the way to Utah!"

Suddenly, all five came back into the clearing with fresh horses.

"Well," J. T. laughed, "the old man felt mighty bad about givin' up such fine animals."

"Yeah," Brushy added, "but he ain't feelin' sorry now. He ain't feelin' nothin'!"

The one called Clayton glanced over at Nathan, and all the men lowered their voices. "You got camp packed up?"

"Yeah, I figured we'll take the roan for a pack horse," one of the men called. "You want me to turn these others out?"

"Nah . . . we'll drive them ahead of us."

"We could shoot them two lame ones," J. T. suggested.

"That might attract buzzards and who knows what else."

"How about the boy?"

"Same thing."

"He'll die all tied up like that," Brushy observed.

"Yeah, but not for a day or two," Clayton replied. "Besides, I'm sure a kid like that can figure out how to get loose sooner or later. Tough luck, boy. You jist came ridin' in to the wrong grove of junipers. But don't fret. When they write the history books, maybe they'll list you as one of the victims of the Blue Mountain Boys."

"Blue Mountain Boys? Is that the gang that goes around killin' children?" Nathan hollered.

Riggins, you jerk, why did you say that?

"I don't need no lip." Clayton pulled his revolver and pointed it at Nathan.

Expecting the sound of gunshot and piercing pain, Nathan grimaced. He heard a completely different sound.

"Well! There you are, Nathan T. Riggins! Try to ride out on me, will you? I'm certainly glad you men hogtied him! I would have done the same thing myself, but it didn't seem ladylike!"

Nathan's mouth dropped open as he saw Leah ride into the clearing. He noticed several guns yanked from holsters and pointed at her.

"I ought to jist leave you out here. It would serve you right! But I don't know how to find my way home. Besides, when my brothers get ahold of you, you'll wish you was tied to a rope and dragged all the way to Wyoming!"

Brothers?

"Who are you?" Clayton huffed.

"Well, until an hour ago I thought I was his girlfriend. Do you know what he did? Did he tell you? I don't suppose so! Well, he invites me out here for a ride in the country and a picnic. Don't that sound nice? I thought it sounded mighty swell.

He says he's got to talk to me about something important. Do you know what it was he wanted to talk about?

"I'll tell you what it was. He up and tells me he don't want to be my boyfriend. Says he likes that Tashawna girl. Do you know her? She's got that stringy, curly hair that looks like a matted cow's tail. She's as skinny as a fence post to boot! Now I ask you, isn't that a fine thing for a boy to do? There are lots of boys in Galena who think I'm quite the looker, Mr. Nathan T. Riggins! Mister, I ain't all that bad-lookin', am I?"

"What's goin' on here?" Clayton mumbled.

"Then he leaves me there cryin' and says he's goin' to hunt some antelope. I ain't seen no antelope out here. Have you men seen any antelope? Of course not! He was just tryin' to dump me. Can you imagine anyone so vile as that? We get back to Galena, and my daddy's goin' to whip you, boy. He'll whip you until you got to stand in the stirrups 'til Christmas."

She's bluffin' them! You can do it, Leah!

"But that ain't nothin' compared to what my brothers will do." Then she turned to Clayton. "They is kinda hot-tempered, you know what I mean? They ain't all that smart, but they kin shoot a lizard from a hundred yards. I've seen 'em do it." Then she turned back to Nathan. "And if you don't git me back home soon, they'll be ridin' out here after me. You know that, don't ya? Mister, kin ya jist unfasten him from the tree and leave him tied up? I'm goin' make him walk all the way back to Galena. I don't care if it takes all day. There ain't no boy alive who can jist dump me like that for no Tashawna."

"You want me to tie her up, too?" J. T. offered.

"Of course he don't want you to tie me up," she protested. "Could you men tell me the direction of Galena? This here boy got me all turned around. I think he's kind of lost, too. He told me that Galena was out there somewhere." Leah waved toward the west. "But I think it's this way, right?" She pointed south.

A wide smile broke across Clayton's face. "That's right, darlin', that's the way home, and don't let this rascal tell you otherwise."

"See there. I told you I could find my way home." She turned and stuck out her tongue at Nathan. Then she looked back at the man. "Thanks, mister, I'm much obliged."

"Cut him loose, but leave his hands tied," Clayton commanded.

Leah bowed her head. "Thank you kindly. I tell you, I learned my lesson good. I ain't ever goin' to ride out in the country with some boy who wants to talk to me. If he cain't tell me right there in the middle of Main Street, I don't want to hear. No, sir, you ain't goin' treat me that way no more."

Nathan pretended to protest. "You aren't going to turn me over to her!"

While cutting the rope around the tree, J. T. laughed. "Yeah, Clayton, we ought to show this boy some mercy. Let's just shoot him and take him out of his misery."

The men laughed as the last of them mounted their horses.

"I don't envy you, boy," Brushy called out as they rode up the mountain toward the east.

Nathan and Leah watched the men until they were out of earshot.

"You did it!" Nathan called out. "Those are the bank robbers! They shot the sheriff down in Austin, and you talked 'em out of shooting me."

Leah took a big, deep breath and sighed. "Yeah . . . I did,

didn't I? I guess I'm good at somethin', Mr. Nathan T. Riggins."

"I thought he was goin' to shoot me."

"Yeah, so did I."

"They could have shot you, too," he reminded her.

"I know."

"Why did you take a chance?" Nathan asked.

"I got lost in the trees and followed them three to this clearin'. When I saw what was happenin', I prayed real hard for the Lord to show me what to do."

"And what did He tell you?"

"He told me that there was worse things than dyin' alongside a good friend."

"I'm sure glad you listened to Him. Where did you come up with that story about brothers and all?"

"Well, I tried to think of something without lyin', but I couldn't think fast enough. I jist couldn't think of nothin' else. The Lord will forgive me for lyin', won't He?"

"If you ask Him, He'll forgive you for anything. You know that. Now, how about climbing off that mare and untying me. I've got to go find Onepenny."

"I tied him up behind that rock pile down yonder. I was afraid they might try to steal him."

"Great! You thought of everything! I can't believe this. You saved Onepenny, too. Now, come on, untie me," Nathan insisted.

"I kind of like havin' a captive audience," she giggled.

"Leah!"

"No, really. If those men turn back, they could see you was loose. We don't want them comin' back now, do we?"

"Leah, you aren't serious. They can't see us from there."

"Maybe they got a spyglass."

"Leah, get down right now and untie me!" Nathan shouted.

"Don't you raise your voice at me. I just might go back to Galena and leave you out here," she threatened.

"Leah, come on, a joke's a joke. Untie me!"

"Not until we get to the rock pile." She slid down off her horse, picked up his carbine, and then remounted the white mare.

"Okay, Riggins, start hikin'," she ordered.

Nathan began to trudge out toward the rock pile.

"When are you movin' anyway?" he teased.

"Keep walkin', Riggins! I ain't ever had a boy all tied up before."

"You aren't goin' to tell people in town about this, are you?"

"Maybe I am, and maybe I ain't." She smiled.

"Look." He motioned with his head. "They're clear over that mountain now. They can't possibly see us. Untie me!"

"I ain't untyin' you until we get to them rocks!"

And she didn't.

■

Finally, mounted on Onepenny, Nathan spurred the spotted horse toward the west.

"How come you keep lookin' back?" Leah asked.

"'Cause I keep having this feeling that they're going to change their minds and come riding after us. I can't believe you talked them into letting us go."

"Well, it's a cinch you weren't doin' too good, them pointin' the pistol at you and all. What do we do now?"

"I've got to get word to Dad. They're heading out through Eureka and Elko Counties. Maybe he can wire ahead and have someone cut them off before they get to the White Desert. Once they get out there, no one will find them."

"Are you sure they're goin' to go east?"

"Wouldn't you?" Nathan asked.

"Yeah . . . I guess so. Is it goin' to be dark before we get home?"

Nathan scanned the sky. "I reckon."

■

The sun had dropped behind the western mountains when they stopped to water their horses at Rabbit Springs. It was dark enough to see the lights of Galena on the distant mountain slope as they trudged across the valley floor. Nathan could feel the hot summer air begin to cool at their 4,000-foot elevation. He pushed his hat back and let it dangle by the stampede string. Then he picked up Onepenny's gait to a lope.

Lord, there for a while I sure didn't think I'd be coming home tonight. You sure did send Leah at the right time. Thanks!

"Nathan?"

"Yeah?"

"You goin' to go back out and help your daddy chase down them bank robbers?"

"Eh . . . no," Nathan admitted. "I've had all I want of that bunch. I don't aim to be that scared again for a long, long time."

"Do you think they had the money from Colin's daddy's bank right there in camp with them?" she asked.

Nathan slowed down the pace of the horses as they started the climb up to Galena.

"I never thought about it much. But I imagine they did. Sometimes I read about outlaws burying their take, but that never seemed too smart to me."

"I miss Colin, but I was kind of glad he wasn't out there with us. That ain't very nice to say, is it?"

Nathan grinned at Leah. "Oh, I know what you mean. Colin doesn't always know the right thing to say." He took a deep breath and sighed. "I miss him, too."

"You know what, Mr. Nathan T. Riggins? We carried on all afternoon and hardly talked about me movin' at all."

"That was nice, wasn't it?" Nathan sighed.

"Yep. And who's going to take care of you when I'm gone? You're liable to get yourself shot without me around," she bragged.

"Oh, I suppose some pretty girl with curly hair will move to town and feel real sorry for me," he teased.

Nathan didn't see Leah swing the canteen until it hit him in the stomach. He bounced back over the cantle and would have tumbled off the horse if Onepenny, sensing trouble, hadn't shut it down and come to a sliding halt.

"Don't you ever go teasin' about other girls, Nathan T. Riggins!" she hollered. Then she kicked the mare and galloped on into Galena.

By the time he reached the livery, Leah's gray horse was waiting to be groomed, but she was nowhere in sight. Nathan hurried through the chores and put up the horses. Then he sprinted home.

Nathan spent a full hour telling his startled and anxious mother everything that had happened with the Blue Mountain Boys. After he ate some navy bean soup and a handful of gingersnaps, he went to the Express Office to send his father a telegram.

He found the front door locked and the "closed" sign posted. Scooting around to the back door, Nathan yelled in through a screened window, "Mr. Fernandez? It's me, Nathan Riggins. I need to send a telegram."

"We're closed up, son."

"This is an emergency!" Nathan called.

"Everyone has an emergency. I'm just sittin' down to eat my supper. Come back in a half-hour if it's still an emergency," the agent hollered.

"But I've got to let Dad know that the bank robbers aren't down in Austin anymore. They're out on the other side of Rabbit Springs."

Suddenly Mr. Fernandez popped his head out the door. "Are they headed this way?" he asked.

"No, they're going east into Utah Territory. That's why I've got to reach my father. Maybe he can get someone to stop them."

"You sure it's them bank robbers?" Mr. Fernandez quizzed.

"Yep. It's the Blue Mountain Boys. You ever heard of them?"

"My word, there's a sizable reward posted for them! . . . Come in, come in, come in. Let's see if Richards is still in the office down in Austin.

■

About an hour after the telegram was sent, Mr. Fernandez came puffing up the dimly-lit dirt street where Nathan and his mother sat out on the porch.

"Evenin', ma'am," he began. "I just got word from the marshal . . . I mean, from Mr. Riggins. Thought you should see this." He handed the telegram to Adele Riggins and then turned to Nathan. "Your daddy and a posse are riding all night to get here. They aim to track those bank robbers themselves!"

8

Deputy Riggins and six well-armed men rode into Galena about ten o'clock the next morning. Nathan and Leah described all the events of the previous afternoon, including details about the men and horses.

"You going to chase them all the way to U. T.?" Nathan asked.

Mr. Riggins put his arm around Nathan's shoulder. "Well, I hope not. The sheriff up in Elko County is sweeping down this way with a posse. We hope to trap them in the middle somewhere, but they've got a good head start."

Nathan walked his father to the front door of the house. "But they're pushing that remuda. Won't that make it easy to track?"

"Sure, we can follow a band of horses. But they can drop off one at a time, and it would be hard to spot. Then if we get close, they can scatter the whole bunch, and we'd have to be mighty smart to know which tracks to follow."

Mr. Riggins glanced back at Leah, then at Nathan. "Now I don't want you two riding off to Rabbit Springs until this matter is settled."

"Eh . . . no, sir, we won't," Nathan assured him. "I don't feel much like leavin' town for a while."

Mr. Riggins grinned. "If you do have to ride off, be sure

and take pretty Miss Leah with you so she can get you out of trouble."

Leah broke into a wide smile.

"Well . . . actually . . . I could have . . . it was just . . . I, eh," Nathan stammered. His father jammed on his hat, stooped to kiss his wife, and then pushed his way through the front door.

"Now don't you go anywhere without 'pretty Miss Leah,'" Leah teased. "You ever notice how your daddy calls me pretty? Maybe there's still hope you'll turn out to be like him."

"I'm going to go feed my hawk and tend the horses. Does 'pretty Miss Leah' want to come with me?"

"It ain't sayin' it that counts," she scolded. "It's how you say it. Your daddy knows how to say it and make a girl feel good. But I'll go. Someone's got to look after you."

"Oh, brother, am I goin' hear that the rest of my life?"

"Nope. Jist for two more weeks," Leah reminded him.

It was almost noon when they hiked up to the Heartford to look for the hawk.

"Domingo! *Venga aquí.*" Nathan searched the sky. "I don't see him. Do you?"

"There ain't no bird on the hotel, I can tell you that much," Leah replied.

"He's not on top the privy either. He's got to be here. It's time to feed him. He wouldn't miss a meal. Maybe someone else came to feed him."

"And maybe he moved to Carson City," Leah teased.

Nathan continued to search the sky. "He's not goin' to leave a good deal."

"I don't know what's such a good deal about gettin' locked into a hotel room."

"Oh, he'll be back by afternoon. You wait and see."

"Well, I ain't goin' to wait right here. Let's go see if the mail's got put up yet," Leah suggested.

Nathan snatched up a pebble and chucked it up the hill. "Does, eh . . . 'pretty Miss Leah' want to race to the post office?"

She lifted her nose. "Ladies don't go runnin' down city streets." Then she spun on her heels and slammed the palms of both hands against Nathan's shoulders, causing him to stagger back and fall to one knee. "But girls do!" she shouted. She hiked her dress above her ankles and raced up the street.

"That's cheating! That's cheating, and you know it," Nathan hollered. By the time he started to sprint, Leah had turned the corner on Main Street, her long brown hair flowing behind her. Nathan didn't try to catch up, but slowed to a walk instead. As he passed the Mercantile, he noticed a full freight wagon parked out front.

"Tony, did Mr. Anderson get some new goods?"

"They ain't comin' in, Nate. It's all goin' out. A fella's openin' a store up in Idaho."

"That's a big sale."

"Mr. Anderson's sellin' out, Nate," Tony explained.

"You mean he's quittin' business?"

"Yep. Says he's goin' to retire in San Diego."

"The Merc's closing? Really?"

"That's the way it goes." Tony shrugged.

Leah was sitting on a bench in front of the post office holding some mail.

"Did you know the Mercantile is closing?" he asked.

"That ain't all that's closin'," she sighed. "Read this."

Nathan unfolded the letter and turned it so that reflected sunlight struck the page.

"Miss D'Imperio? She's not coming back! She's goin' to teach in St. Louis this year? But . . . but we . . ."

"She don't think they'll even have a school in Galena," Leah reported. "It's all over, ain't it, Nathan? I guess maybe it's time for us all to move on."

"Well, you aren't moving for two weeks, so I'm not going to get sad 'til then."

Leah glanced up at Nathan. "Will you be sad then?"

"Yeah," Nathan said softly, "I don't think I will want to live here anymore either." He stared down Main Street. "Hey, what's going on over at the bank?"

"Mr. Melton is goin' to pay folks off, I think. Ain't that what Colin's daddy said?" Leah glanced down at her lap. "Colin! I almost forgot . . . You got a letter."

"Already? But he's only been gone—"

"Read it to me!" She handed him the slick brown envelope.

Dear Nathan,

We are here in Carson City. Father is settling up financial matters. He says Mr. Melton should soon have enough money to reconcile all accounts in Galena. I think perhaps we might buy a house here. Father has been offered a nice position with the U. S. Mint, and mother has some family in Virginia City.

Guess who I saw today? Tashawna! She wanted to know how you were doing. (Maybe you'd better not let Leah read this.) She promised to show me all over town. You should see her. She really, you know, grew up.

Please try to come to Carson City this summer.
I'd really like to see you. (And so would Tashawna.)
Say hello to Tona and Leah for me.

Your friend,
Colin Maddison, Jr.

"You ain't goin' to Carson, Mr. Nathan T. Riggins. If Colin wants to see you, he can just come to Galena . . . or wherever. 'Say hello to Tona and Leah'?" she mimicked. "I get mentioned down there with the dog!"

"Let's go see Mr. Melton. Maybe he knows if the Maddisons plan on coming back any time soon." Nathan sprinted across the dusty dirt street and then spun around and ran back to Leah.

"I'm not in that big a hurry," he sheepishly admitted. "If you promise not to push me down, I'll walk with you."

"I ain't promisin' nothin'." Leah grinned. She stepped out into the street with her head tilted slightly upward. "Hey, is that your old hawk up there?"

"Where?"

"Way up there." She pointed high in the blue sky above the Mercantile.

"Yeah . . . it's a hawk all right! That must be him. That's Domingo!"

"How can you tell from here?" she questioned.

"I'll show you. I'll whistle him in." Nathan pulled the heavy leather glove out of his back pocket and slipped it over his left hand. Even though Nathan's whistle was loud and shrill, the hawk continued to circle.

"That ain't him," Leah decided.

"It is too. He'll come. Just wait."

"Well, if it is, he jist flew off toward them mountains."

"But . . . but . . . maybe he didn't know it was me."

"And maybe, Mr. Nathan T. Riggins, that ain't your old hawk in the first place."

Nathan searched the sky for another glimpse of the bird. "Maybe you're right," he mumbled. "Maybe that wasn't Domingo. He wouldn't just fly off."

Mr. Watson was helping two men wearing double Colts unload a couple of locked metal boxes when Nathan and Leah walked up.

"Is that a shipment from Mr. Maddison?" Nathan asked.

"Oh, Nathan . . . yes, it is. Say, did I hear that your daddy got back in town this morning?"

"Yeah, but he already rode off with a posse after the bank robbers," Nathan reported.

"Are they around here?"

"They're out in the Shoshones headed toward Utah Territory."

"That is some comfort." Mr. Melton wiped the sweat off his forehead. "Although I'd feel better if your dad were in town."

"What's the matter? You ain't expectin' no trouble, are you?" Leah quizzed.

"No . . . no, not really. It's just . . . well, the safe is all busted up, and I'll have to baby-sit these funds until everyone comes in to collect. By noon tomorrow everything should be reconciled."

"You goin' to stay here until then?" Leah asked.

"Yes, I see no other option."

"Kin we bring you some dinner and supper? I'm stayin' with Nathan's mama, and she's one of the best cooks in town."

"That's mighty kind of you, Miss Leah. I'd be obliged. And say . . . if you two happen to see any suspicious types hanging around town, let me know. The Maddisons had to go into debt to raise these funds, you know. But that's the way they are. They pay their debts."

"Are you open for business now?" Nathan asked.

"Not 'til mornin'," Mr. Watson replied. "I've got to get the paperwork done."

"Mr. Watson, do you know if the Maddisons will be coming back to see that everything is taken care of?"

"I don't think so, son."

"We'll bring you some dinner after a while," Leah promised.

"Thank you, Miss Leah."

Leah and Nathan hiked home.

"It don't seem fair. Them robbers take all the money, and Mr. Maddison has to pay it off. Some bankers would just ride off and forget Galena," Leah noted.

"Nobody but a thief would do that. A man pays his debts. That's the code," Nathan replied.

"What code?"

"Well . . . you know. It's just the way good folks operate out here. You know . . . the code."

"I don't think I'm goin' to marry a banker. That Tashawna can marry the banker. Now wouldn't that be a pair? Mr. and Mrs. Colin Maddison (with two *d*'s), Jr. He could make the money, and she could spend it."

Nathan turned to Leah with a wide grin. "Hey, that does sound fine, doesn't it? Then every time we went to visit Colin, we could—"

"Forget it, Riggins! I ain't ever goin' to visit her, even if I'm an old lady."

"Now, now, pretty Miss Leah. I think you'd better learn to be more trusting."

"And I think you better figure out which subjects not to tease about," she huffed.

■

All the rest of the day, Leah and Nathan got along fine, providing they didn't talk about moving or a girl whose name started with T. That evening after a supper of fried steak, boiled red potatoes, and applesauce, Mrs. Riggins, Leah, and Nathan sat out on the porch.

"It isn't coolin' off much tonight, is it?" Mrs. Riggins commented.

"Nope, it's almost hot enough to soak the sheets," Leah offered.

"Do what?" Nathan asked.

"One summer we lived down in west Texas, and it was so hot at night we pulled our beds right out on the porch. But we still couldn't sleep, so my daddy soaked a sheet in cold water and then wrung it out real good. We pulled it over us, and we went right to sleep . . . until the sheet dried out, of course."

"Did you have to do that all summer long?" Mrs. Riggins asked.

"Nah. We didn't stay there that long. We moved to Lincoln, New Mexico . . . but it weren't no better there in the summer." Leah reached out and scratched Tona's head as he sat in front of her.

"Look at that!" Nathan motioned to his mother. "Tona sure does pick up with Leah around. I think he's feelin' better . . . don't you?"

"Well, he's certainly more active. Maybe you two could take him for a little hunt tomorrow. Just up behind town. If he got tired, it would be a downhill walk all the way home," Mrs. Riggins suggested.

"I ain't goin' very far away from town. I got all the scare I wanted yesterday," Leah declared.

"Let's get up real early and hike up toward the old Copper Basin mine. There's always some rabbits up there," Nathan suggested.

"How early is early?" Leah demanded.

"Oh . . . daylight."

"How much daylight?"

"Breakin' daylight."

"Oh, all right. I ain't never went for a walk with a boy at daybreak."

"Well, it's not exactly a walk," Nathan protested.

"It ain't? You mean we got to run?"

"No . . . what I mean, it's a huntin' trip where we walk, but it's not a . . . you know, a walk."

■

Nathan was on the front porch the next morning scrubbing his face at a wash basin when Leah came out.

"Ain't you ready yet?"

"I thought you'd need . . . a little more time," Nathan stammered, drying his face.

"Well, you thought wrong," she asserted. "Tona! That-a-boy! Come on. Let's walk down and feed the horses while we're waiting for slowpoke."

"Slowpoke? I'm ready! I just need to pull on my boots,

grab my hat, my carbine, a handful of shells, and maybe some biscuits."

"I have the biscuits!" she announced. "Me and Tona will be down at the livery."

Nathan ran back into the house, put on his boots, grabbed his carbine, and then took five minutes looking for a dozen .44-40 cartridges to shove into his pocket.

By the time he reached the livery, Leah had pulled down the hay and was holding an oat bucket for Onepenny.

"He sure is a purdy horse. I'm goin' to miss him, too."

"You aren't going to start the day sad, are you?" Nathan asked.

"Nope. Let's go shoot a snake or rabbit or somethin' ferocious."

Nathan was surprised that Tona traipsed up the hill well ahead of them. He never got out of sight, but he only slightly limped, and his eyes seemed to perk up.

"He's definitely feeling better," Nathan remarked.

They roamed up the hill about two hundred yards above the town and then headed west along the slope of the mountain. They walked slowly, visiting as they hiked. Tona stayed about twenty feet ahead of them. Nathan carried the carbine, loaded with three shells, over his shoulders, with each arm resting on the gun.

The sunlight just creased the top of the mountains, and Nathan watched it gradually slide down the hill until they walked in daylight. He figured daybreak in the summer was the best time of the day in northern Nevada. Looking south, he could see mountains one hundred and fifty miles away.

"I ain't seen nothin' to shoot," Leah complained.

"It doesn't matter." Nathan shrugged. "It's mainly just a

walk for Tona. Hey, let's sit on these rocks and have a biscuit. Tona! Come here, boy," he called.

They sat on the rocks and ate biscuits and salt pork. Tona sniffed around the sagebrush and disappeared.

Leah nodded toward Galena. "If we had a spyglass, we could sit here and watch what was going on in town."

"Yeah . . ." Nathan gazed off at the western mountains and then back at Galena. "Most of the time it's a windy, barren spot up here. I mean, if it weren't for gold, no one would ever want to live in this country."

"What do you think will happen to town?" Leah asked.

"Oh, a few will hang on for a while . . . they might even open the Shiloh again. But sooner or later it will look like Willow Springs. Empty buildings without window casings or doors. Snow and rain blowing through rooms. Then one day it'll catch fire and burn to the ground. The ashes will drift away; the sage will grow back . . . and by 1910 nobody will even remember there was a town here."

"Boy, that ain't very cheerful."

Nathan climbed up on the rocks and looked around for Tona.

"Well, I guess I'm kind of in a sad mood. It might not be that depressing."

"Sort of reminds me of some folks' lives."

"What does?"

"You know, their lives just sort of flash by. Then they die, and nobody remembers that they were even around. You ever notice how many markers in the cemetery don't have a name on them?"

"Yeah . . . well, it doesn't have to be that way. I think the Lord has more in mind for us than that."

"Nathan, do you ever think about Heaven?"

"Sometimes . . . how about you?"

"Yep. I think about it all the time. Sometimes I wish we could hurry up and get there," Leah said pondering. "Is it true that there ain't no marriage in Heaven?"

"That's what I read in the Bible." Nathan nodded.

She grinned. "Well . . . well, I think maybe I'll wait a few years before goin' there."

"Hey!" Nathan shouted. "Tona's found a rabbit!" He quickly cocked his carbine and, looking down the metal sights, followed the darting jackrabbit as it scampered several feet in front of a puffing Tona.

Squeezing the trigger, Nathan heard the report, felt the kick, and saw the rabbit turn a somersault and fall lifeless on the mountainside.

"You got it!" Leah shouted.

"Yeah, it's kind of a big bullet for the target." Nathan shrugged. "Look at Tona pounce on it! You'd think he was a pup."

The dog carried the rabbit in his teeth and began to trot back to town.

"I think Tona's through huntin'," Leah remarked.

"How about you?" Nathan asked. "You want to go back to town now?"

"Sure. Your mama promised to show me how to bake some french pastries. And we ought to take Mr. Melton some breakfast."

■

As they hiked down the hill, Nathan noticed that Tona

often stopped and dropped the rabbit, caught his breath, then picked up the animal, and continued the descent.

They were within a hundred feet of town when Leah called out, "Hey . . . ain't that an open window at the Heartford Hotel?"

"What window?" Nathan asked.

"The one in the corner. It's a little bit open at the top . . . see? Maybe a couple, three inches or so. Didn't you close it the other day?"

"No, I didn't close it. I didn't even know it was open. I guess I was so excited to find Domingo that I—" Nathan stopped suddenly. "Domingo! He could have crawled back in that room and now can't get out! That's it. I bet he's stuck back in the hotel. Let's go check it out."

"I ain't crawlin' into no boarded-up hotel. Me and Tona and what's left of the rabbit will wait out here."

"I'll be right back. Hold my carbine. I know he's in there."

Nathan ran to the back of the hotel and lifted the window. He pulled himself into the musty kitchen and scooted through the darkened lobby of the hotel.

"Domingo?" he shouted as he ran up the stairs. "Hey, Domingo, are you stuck again?"

He shoved open the door of the corner room and scampered toward the slightly open window.

Suddenly someone grabbed the collar of his shirt, and he felt a revolver pressed to his back.

"Well, well, boys, look at this," a gruff but familiar voice snarled. "If it ain't the horse-stealin' antelope hunter himself!"

9

Nathan swallowed hard and gasped, "The Blue Mountain Boys!"

"Ain't that nice? The boy remembers who we are." Clayton snarled, "I should of plugged him out at Rabbit Springs."

"Don't shoot him in here," J. T. warned. "A shot might bring the whole town out."

"This town ain't that quiet, is it?"

J. T. walked over and glanced out the window. "Well, it surely ain't boisterous like the old days. You can hear dogs bark clean across town."

"I still figure most every man with nerve enough to pull a trigger is in that posse out chasin' our remuda."

Regaining his breath, Nathan glanced around the darkened room and could spot only four of the five men. "What are you doin' here? I thought you were headed to Utah."

"Yeah, that's exactly what we wanted you to think. Then you'd come runnin' back to Galena and send the authorities out after us," Clayton reported.

"Then," Brushy continued, "while all the law is out chasin' Wesley and that band of horses, we slip into town and scoop up anything that's left over from the other day."

"Tie him up, J. T.!" Clayton ordered. "You see, kid, that

banker will bring in new funds to pay off his accounts. I know the type—they're fanatic about payin' everyone back. So as soon as they open that door this morning, we'll make a withdrawal."

Don't they know the safe is broken? Or that the Maddisons have left? If they'd known that, they could have broken in last night.

"Yeah, I bet that banker wished he had what's in these saddlebags!" J. T. laughed as he pushed Nathan to the dusty, dirty floor and tied his hands to the bedpost.

They've got the bank money here? Dad and the posse could be a hundred miles away by now!

Clayton tramped over to the corner window and glanced down toward the bank.

"I cain't figure why that banker hasn't showed up."

"Them banks don't open until late," Brushy mumbled.

"But he's got to come down and set things up for the day," Clayton reasoned.

"The bank's closed," Nathan shouted out. "The Maddisons moved to Carson City."

Why did I say that?

"Closed?" J. T. snapped. "That ain't the way I heard it at the Drover's Cafe. They said the bank's goin' to open this mornin' to pay folks off."

"But if it ain't the banker, who are we lookin' fer?" Brushy questioned.

"Well, I can tell you one thing," Clayton announced, "the first person that walks through that door who knows the combination to the safe is goin' to get some visitors real quick like." Then turning again to Nathan, he demanded, "What were you doin' in the Heartford anyway?"

"I was, ah . . . hunting for my hawk."

"Hawk? Nobody owns a hawk." Brushy laughed.

"That hawk that flew in here last week? It was yours?" Clayton asked.

"Uh . . . that's the one. Is it in here again?"

"Nah, we ain't seen him this time," J. T. began. "Clayton! Come here! Folks are headin' into the bank."

"Folks?"

"Yeah . . . ordinary town people."

Clayton stormed to the window and glanced down at Galena's Main Street. "How'd we miss the banker? Well, boys, let's get down there before they give away all our money. Brushy, gather up those saddlebags and, Milt, you bring the horses around."

"We ain't comin' back here?"

"Nope, not with this kid snoopin' around. J. T., stick a gag in his mouth. Boys, we've got to move smooth, and we've got to move fast. If someone gets in your way, shoot 'em."

"Ain't nobody goin' to shoot nobody!"

Nathan and the men looked up to see Leah, with Tona by her side, standing in the doorway holding Nathan's .44-40 carbine.

"Leah!"

"Oh, no, not that mouthy girl! Don't you ever git tired of buttin' in?"

"You untie Nathan, or one of ya is gettin' blasted!"

"That's it. I've had it. Kids ain't got no respect anymore." Clayton reached up and pulled his black hat down tighter.

"I ain't bluffin', mister. I'll pull this trigger! Tell 'em, Nathan. Tell 'em I ain't bluffin'!"

"Leah, run! Warn Mr. Melton that they intend to rob the bank again!" Nathan shouted.

"Ain't nobody goin' nowhere!" Clayton marched straight at Leah.

Lord, save Leah! Don't let her get hurt!

When Clayton came within five steps of Leah, he reached to his side to pull out his revolver. Suddenly, Tona let out a deep growl and leaped at Clayton's right arm. His teeth had just broke skin when Clayton let out a yell, dropped his gun, and slung the dog to the floor.

Immediately, Brushy whipped out his Colt and shot Tona. The gray and white dog fell dead after the first shot. There was no response when the second shot punctured his body.

"No!" Nathan yelled.

"Tona!" Leah screamed.

Clayton lunged at Leah and grabbed the carbine. The gun discharged wildly and shattered the hotel window. The other men dived for cover. Then Clayton shoved Leah into the middle of the room. She tripped over Tona's body and fell to the floor beside Nathan.

"Why did you do that? Why did you kill my dog?" Nathan cried. He could feel the tears streaming down his face. He was trying to catch his breath, but the sobs grew uncontrollable. He tried to pull free from the bindings but only managed to hurt himself more.

"I'm sorry, Nathan. I'm sorry," Leah wailed. "I shouldn't have brought Tona up here. It's all my fault! I'm sorry . . . oh, Lord, I feel so bad I want to die!"

"Clayton! There's some folks headin' this way. They must have heard them shots!"

"Tie her up with the boy. Milt, run get the horses and bring them around back. Let's get out of here."

"How about the bank?"

"Forget it. The odds just switched, and it ain't worth gettin' killed over. There'll be other banks."

The tall man called Milt ran out the door, and Nathan could hear his boots tramp down the hallway. Then they heard several shots. Clayton stuck his head out the doorway.

"Milt, what's wrong?"

"They were takin' down the boards over the front door. But that should cause them to think again."

"How about in the back?" Nathan heard Clayton shout.

Two more shots blasted from somewhere downstairs.

"They've got us surrounded, boys. We'll have to shoot our way out. Come on downstairs, and we'll try to break through."

"How about these kids?" J. T. called as he scooped up the saddlebags with the bank money.

"Leave 'em tied. We might need them alive later on."

"Well, I ain't leavin' this carbine again!" J. T. scooped up the gun and ran out of the room, slamming the door. Someone locked it.

A few more shouts and two more gunshots . . . then silence from downstairs.

The gunfire had diverted Nathan's attention. He finally had control of his sobbing. He glanced at Tona's lifeless body and then over at Leah who hung her head down. He could see tears dripping onto her dress.

"Leah? Leah . . . it's okay . . . Leah . . . please stop crying," Nathan tried to comfort her.

He heard her sobs lessen. Finally she lifted her head and

took a deep breath. Still not looking at Nathan, she spoke in a slow, soft voice.

"He wanted to come in . . . honest, Nathan."

"What?"

"Tona," she explained. "You know how he don't like to ever go into buildings? Well, you was gone so long that Tona barked and barked at that kitchen window. I ain't heard him bark that much in a year. Did you hear him?"

"Eh . . . no, I guess not . . . well, maybe."

Nathan heard shouting from somewhere down in the street. Then the men downstairs yelled something in return.

"What's happening?" Leah asked.

"Sounds like the people in town have the hotel surrounded. They must have heard the shots."

"What people? Your daddy's out there chasin' . . . chasin' that band of horses, I guess."

"Harris Anderson, Brady Wheeler, Tony, and Briggs at the freight office, Mr. Fernandez—men like that."

They both sat silent for a few minutes listening.

Finally, it was Leah who spoke up. "Nathan?"

"Yeah."

"It breaks my heart to see Tona layin' there. You know that, don't ya?"

"Yeah. I hurt real bad, too."

"You know what I think?" she continued. "I think shootin' Tona might have saved the bank from being robbed again."

"It might be that they won't even get away with the money they stole in the first place," Nathan added.

Tear streaks had dried on her face. "That sort of makes him the town hero, don't it?"

"Yeah . . . you're right!" Nathan took a deep breath of the dusty, stale air in the hotel room.

"See, Tona started barking, and when I climbed into the kitchen to come look you up, he pitched such a fit I had to bring him along . . . really! Do you think he knew you was in trouble?"

"I don't know, but . . . wait . . . did you hear what they shouted? I think they mentioned us."

"They goin' to shoot us?" Leah asked.

A gunshot punctuated her sentence. The two waited a long time before speaking. Finally, Leah whispered, "What are you thinkin' about?"

"I guess I was kind of prayin' about Tona, you know, asking God why this had to happen."

"What did He say?"

Nathan waited a minute. Two of the bank robbers argued with each other down in the lobby.

"Well, I don't know if it was the Lord. But I got to thinking about how much Tona's been hurting lately—ever since the bobcat tore him up. Well, I don't think he's had a good day since last summer . . . until today."

"You call gettin' shot a good day?" Leah tugged at the curtain sash that tied her hands.

"Tona got to go huntin'. He got to tote a rabbit home, and he died." Nathan could feel the tears rolling down his face again. The knot in his throat made it hard to talk. "Leah, he died doing exactly what he liked doing best, protecting me and you. The first time I met Tona, he saved me from that crazy bear up at Willow Springs. Huntin' and protectin'—I think it was better than slowly dyin' in pain on the front step."

They both stared at the lifeless Tona and listened again to the argument below.

"We've got to get out of here!" Nathan tried fumbling with the knot. "They'll get around to using us as shields to make a break for the horses. Leah, it looks like they just tied your hands behind the bedpost. Can you slide down the post and scoot out from under it?"

"I can't lift the bed."

"Maybe I can lift the whole bed. Then you see if you can slip out."

Nathan twisted himself around to an awkward position and placed his shoulders under the frame of the hotel bed. By shoving straight up, he was able to raise the bed a couple of inches.

"Quick . . . there . . . hurry . . . I can't hold it much longer!"

"I'm hurryin', Nathan. I'm hurryin' . . . I can't get loose . . . I can't!"

"Try!" Nathan insisted.

Suddenly, Leah's ropes popped off the bedpost. "There! I did it!"

"Someone's coming!" Nathan whispered. "Sit back down. Quick! Pretend you're still tied to the bedpost."

Clayton unlocked the door and burst into the room with his Colt .44 held tight in his right hand. "What's all the noise up here?" he shouted.

"It was me," Nathan announced. "She's drivin' me crazy with all her talk. Can't you put me in another room so I don't have to listen to this?"

"We could toss you out this second-story window," Clayton sneered. "If you two make another fuss, I'll gag you both!" He walked over to the corner window. "Ain't that somethin'? I didn't reckon there were that many folks left in this town. There must be a hundred folks down there. Most of 'em pointin' guns. I don't know how they got down here so blamed fast!"

"What are you goin' to do with us?" Leah asked.

"Well, don't worry none for a while. As long as you sit tight, we ain't goin' to do nothin'. Once we told them folks we had you two in here, we got them scared of shootin' just in case they hit you. So we'll just hole up 'til dark. Then we'll let you help us escape."

"We ain't goin' to help you," Leah protested.

"Darlin', you'll help. All I have to do is stuff a rag in your mouth and tote you right in front of me to stop bullets."

"Don't you ever call me darlin'!" she fired back.

"Girly, I'll call you—"

A shout from down below ended his sentence. Clayton hustled out the door and tramped down the stairs.

"Leah, can you scoot over here and untie me?" Nathan asked.

"My hands is tied tight. I cain't get down under that bed and untie nothin'."

She awkwardly struggled to her feet and walked softly over toward the window. After glancing out, she scooted back to Nathan.

"They got wagons and rigs and people all over down there!"

"Well, don't get too close to the window. If folks see you and cause a ruckus, the robbers will see it and come running up the stairs before we figure out how to get out of here. We've got to get untied."

"There's some scissors on this dresser," Leah announced. "But I don't rightly see how I can use them behind my back."

"You've got to try," Nathan encouraged her.

Backing up to the mirrored dresser, Leah bent forward and raised her bound arms. Nathan watched as she stood up and attempted to cut the rope.

"Come on, Leah! We've got to hurry. They could be coming back up here any time!"

"I'm hurryin'! Oh!" she cried.

"Are you all right?"

"Yeah . . . I'm hurryin' . . . honest, Nathan, I'm hurryin'. There!"

Nathan watched as she pulled her hands around in front of her and pulled off the rest of the curtain sash. Blood oozed down the back of her hand and dripped to the floor.

"You cut yourself."

"Yeah . . . but I hurried."

"Leah, I didn't mean you had to—"

"I been hurt worse." She scooted next to Nathan with the scissors still in her right hand.

"Don't worry, I won't cut you. I can see what I'm doin' now."

"I wasn't worried. I'm . . . I'm sorry for makin' you hurry and cut yourself," he apologized.

"Well, we're both free! Now what?"

Nathan stood and rubbed his wrists. Then he knelt down beside Tona and petted the fur gently.

"We aren't going anywhere without Tona."

"We cain't carry a dead dog."

Nathan glanced up at Leah.

"Oh . . . well, yeah . . . we'll take him. How are we going to carry him?"

"Look in the wardrobe for a box or something." Nathan motioned toward the free-standing closet. "Well, old boy, you've been a good dog . . . and you taught me some things about loyalty and life and . . . Well, you should've picked out some other kid to follow around. Someone smart enough to not let you go chasin' bobcats and bank robbers. But I loved you, Tona." Nathan began to cry. "You know I loved you."

"Nathan," Leah said softly, "there ain't no box, but I did find this valise."

She handed Nathan a medium-sized worn leather suitcase. He gently scooped up Tona and carefully laid him inside the valise. He closed it up and lifted it with his right hand.

"It isn't very heavy. Tona's been awful skinny since last summer," Nathan commented.

"Tona was always skinny." Leah shrugged. "Now where do we go from here? There ain't no outside stairway, is there?"

"I think one of the rooms has a ladder sort of built right on the outside wall. You think you can make it down a tall ladder?"

"I'll make it." She nodded. "Which room is it?"

"One of 'em on that back side."

"How we goin' to get there without being noticed?"

"I don't think they locked the door the last time out, so I think we'd better crawl on our bellies down the hall. Maybe they won't be looking our way."

"If they come chasin' us, what do we do then?"

"Start praying, I guess," Nathan advised.

"Start prayin'? I been prayin' like crazy the whole time."

"Okay, come on! We'll head down the hall into the middle room. No matter what, don't say anything until we get there."

Nathan dropped to his hands and knees and scooted the suitcase with Tona alongside him. Motioning with his hand for Leah to follow, he swung open the door, dropped down to his stomach, and crawled across the hall. He smelled dust and stale liquor. Nathan had almost reached one of the middle rooms on the back side of the landing when he heard voices. Someone was coming up the stairs.

"We got to make a break, J. T. More and more people are comin'. This is suicide sittin' in here."

"Brushy, we bust out now, and we'd be shot down in a minute. Clayton's right."

"I'd rather die in the fresh air with a gun in my hand than be hung by a rope with a bunch of old ladies lookin' on. I'm grabbin' those kids and leavin'. You can stay if you want."

Lord, he's going to see us! No! Help us, Lord, help us!

"Brushy! Come back down here!" J. T. yelled. "We've got to stick together on this thing. Come on, Brushy, you don't want to face them guns by yourself."

Nathan saw the top of the man's hat spin and disappear down the stairs.

"You and me had nothin' to do with shootin' that sheriff. They can't blame us for that one, can they, J. T.?"

"Come on, Brushy. By mornin' we'll be ridin' north to Wyoming. By Friday we'll be playin' Faro in Cheyenne. Just stay by your window and don't let no one go sneakin' up on us."

The distant voices sounded muffled as Nathan shoved open the door of the hotel room and scooted inside. Once Leah made it into the room, he locked the door with a skeleton key that had been left in the lock.

"We made it!" Leah whispered.

"So far," Nathan cautioned.

He stood up and went to the window, peering out on the right side of the dusty lace curtains.

"It's here! There's the ladder!"

Leah glanced out at the people who filled the mountain-side behind the hotel. "How do we get out there?"

"Just open the window and . . . Leah, it's stuck! I can't get the window open!"

"Just beat on it with something. It will open."

"I can't beat on it. Someone downstairs will hear."

Leah stepped over to the corner of the room next to a broken rocking chair.

"Here's a curtain rod." She motioned. "Pry it open with this."

Nathan jammed the rod under the window at the right corner and pushed down on the rod. It began to bend. Then suddenly the window broke free. The wooden-cased window flew wide open and crashed into the side of the hotel with such impact that the glass shattered and tumbled to the ground below.

They heard someone running up the stairs.

10

Leah, you go first. There might not be time for us both to get down."

"You go. I'm scared of them steps. They don't look too safe!"

"You got to do it. Stay close up against the building when you get down there. Then we'll figure out how to get to the wagons! Go on!"

Nathan helped Leah crawl out the window to the ladder steps. They stretched all the way from the ground to the roof of the building.

She clutched each rung with white knuckles and inched her way down the outside of the hotel.

"I'm scared, Nathan!"

"You can do it! Keep going!"

Nathan grabbed up the valise with Tona and placed one foot out on the steps. The one-by-four wooden slats had white paint flaking off, revealing dark gray weathered wood beneath. The suitcase, now swinging on his right arm, seemed unbearably heavy. He heard a loud crash from inside the hotel room. The door swung open.

"Get back in here, kid!" J. T. screamed.

Nathan had descended only a couple of steps. The bank

robber, being careful not to expose himself as a target in front of the window, pointed his Colt right at the boy.

"Crawl back in here or you're dead!" he commanded.

Nathan glanced down. Leah had made it safely to the ground and was scrunched up tight against the side of the hotel, out of sight of the gunmen in the hotel, but in full view of the townspeople.

Without thinking about it, Nathan moaned, "Lord, help me!"

"That's right, boy, say your prayers because if you don't get yourself back in this room, you'll be goin' to meet your Master."

Nathan looked up at the outlaw holding the gun. The man squinted his eyes, making tight creases around them.

"Mister, you men tied me up, threatened me and Leah, robbed a bank or two, stole some horses, shot a sheriff, and killed my dog. You've proved there isn't much about you that's decent. Well, I'm going to find out if you're low enough to kill an unarmed kid while the whole town's looking on 'cause I'm not crawling back in there."

Nathan eased on down the ladder.

Lord, if I got to die, well, I sure hope I can be as brave as Tona.

He heard several shouts and curses, but no shots were fired out the window. By the time he reached the ground, his right arm ached. Sweat dripped off his forehead.

"Were you talkin' to one of them?" Leah asked.

"Yep."

"What did he say?"

"He told me to crawl back in there or he'd shoot."

Leah scooted next to the building and sat in the dirt. Nathan plopped down beside her.

"What did you tell him?"

"I told him I didn't think he was the type to shoot unarmed kids in front of the whole town."

Leah took a deep breath. "Well . . . I guess he wasn't. What are we goin' to do now?"

A roar of noise rose from the townspeople. Several shouted at them to stay put. This was followed by several bursts of gunfire at the front side of the hotel.

"What are they doin' around there?" Leah asked.

"I suppose they're trying to get the bank robbers' attention so we can escape." Nathan searched the distant crowd to see who was among them. Most remained safely hidden from sight. A man inched his way closer to the building. "Tony's trying to get to us!"

"Maybe they're all around front," Leah guessed.

Several rifle shots forced Tony to dive back behind a wagon.

"Then again, maybe they ain't," she added. "Which one was up in that room?"

"The one they call J. T."

"That Clayton fella wasn't in there, was he?"

"Nope."

"Well." Leah took a deep breath. "If J. T. didn't shoot you while you was on the ladder, maybe he won't shoot us if we run for it."

"No, we can't . . ." Nathan heard more gunfire from the front. "Well, maybe . . . just maybe we can. You really want to try it?"

"Do you?" she asked.

"Yeah . . . sort of. Yeah, let's do it!" Nathan maneuvered to his feet but stayed tight against the building. Leah stood alongside and brushed off her dress. Nathan straightened his hat and picked up the valise.

"Which way are we going to run?"

"Straight ahead—toward that freight wagon."

"Together?"

"Yep," Nathan asserted. "But we aren't running. We're going to walk right out there and not look back. If they're going to shoot us, they can do it if we run or walk. I say we walk with our heads up."

Leah looked up at Nathan and scrunched her nose just enough to make the freckles wiggle.

"Will you hold my hand?"

"What?"

"I'll walk by your side if you hold my hand."

"All right." Nathan took another deep breath and then prayed aloud, "Lord, this is Nathan and Leah . . . and we're scared. Walk with us, Jesus. Please walk with us."

Nathan ignored the shouts of the townspeople and began walking toward the freight wagon. Leah laced her fingers into his left hand, and with his right he carried the leather suitcase containing Tona.

Without looking over at Leah, he called out, "Keep your head up."

"My head is up."

"Don't look back."

"I ain't lookin' back."

"Don't get in a hurry."

"I'm not in a hurry!"

Nathan could feel the sweat drip from his forehead. "Just

a few more steps . . . oh, Lord . . . just a few more." When they came close to the wagon, Nathan dragged Leah by the arm and dove to safety.

Suddenly, a throng of townspeople swarmed around them, and a great cheer went up. Leah and Nathan got pulled in two different directions. Mr. Walker was there hugging Leah, and tears streamed down her face.

Nathan felt familiar arms surround him, and he looked up to see his mother's relieved face. Taller than she, he stooped over and laid his head on her shoulder. Finally, regaining her composure, his mother spoke, "Nathan, I was very proud of you. The way you walked out of there, taking care of Leah, and all. It's the kind of thing your father would have done."

"Mama . . . they killed Tona." Nathan started to cry again. Then he stood up and wiped his eyes and looked at all the townspeople staring at them. "He was trying to protect me and Leah, and they shot him twice even though the first bullet killed him. I've got him in the valise."

"In there?" His mother pointed.

"Yep. I wasn't goin' to leave him in the hotel with them."

"I'm really sorry, Nathan." His mother tried to console him.

"It's all right, Mother. Leah and me talked it out . . . and . . . well, I can take it now."

Nathan knew the words sounded right, but tears still streamed down his cheeks.

"Well, come on. We're going to get you home. Your father can take care of this matter now." She tugged him back up the street away from the hotel.

"Daddy's here? But I thought he was—"

"He picked up their trail last night and rode two horses

into the ground getting back. He and the others rode up about the time you started crawling out the window. He's the one who got the diversion going around front. Mr. Walker got back to town this morning, too."

"Yeah, I saw him."

"Are you hungry?" his mother asked.

"Well . . . actually . . . yeah, I am," Nathan admitted.

"I thought so." Mrs. Riggins slipped her arm into Nathan's, and they walked side by side through the crowd of people.

■

Nathan and his mother ate dinner on the front porch while a steady stream of people stopped by to congratulate Nathan for his bravery and bring the latest report from the standoff down at the hotel.

At about three o'clock they heard several rounds of gunfire. Then word came that one of the bank robbers was wounded, and at least two of them wanted to surrender. A few minutes later there was a loud cheer, and Tony ran up to Nathan, who now stood in the street.

"They surrendered to your daddy!" Tony yelled. "It's all over, and the bank got its money back! They got it all back!"

The following hour was a confusion of visits and reports. His mother insisted that Nathan stay near the house. She wouldn't let him out of her sight. His father came home for only a few minutes to announce that he and the posse were immediately hauling the prisoners to Austin.

Nathan hardly had time to hug his father and tell him about Tona.

"You bury him up on the hill, Nate. Don't be leavin' him around here overnight."

"Yes, sir. When will you be back?"

"Can't say. If it's going to be long, I'll send a telegram. Take care of your mother."

"Yes, sir . . . I will."

■

That evening Nathan hiked up the hill behind Galena to a small grove of junipers. In one hand was the suitcase, still containing Tona. In the other was a shovel. For several moments he dug in the rocky ground. The soil was dry and had a yellow tint that made the dust-laden air taste bitter.

He had just finished the hole and was about to lower Tona into it when he heard footsteps and spun around. Leah was standing there wearing a new blue dress.

"Leah! You look . . . I mean, that's a pretty dress."

"Is it respectable if I come to the buryin'?" she asked.

"Sure. I would have gone to get you, but I figured you needed to be with your father."

He lowered the whole suitcase into the hole and began to fill the dirt in over it.

"You buryin' him in that?"

"Yeah, it's like . . . you know, a coffin."

"Ain't you goin' to say no words over him?"

"I'm sort of . . . all cried out." Nathan stopped shoveling. He hiked up his brown duckings, pulled off his hat, and cleared his throat.

"Lord, Tona was a good dog for me. I thank You for the years we had together, but I surely wish he could have stayed around longer. And I do thank You that he isn't hurting any more. In Jesus' name, amen."

"Amen," Leah echoed. "You were right about me needin' to talk to my daddy. We are movin' to Austin, Nathan."

"When?"

"In the mornin'."

Nathan felt a wave of shock sweep through his whole body. "But I thought you had . . . two more weeks."

"Daddy bought a barber shop, and he wants to open up the day after tomorrow. So we're startin' to load up things in a wagon. Daddy said you can come help load if you have a mind to."

■

For the next two hours Nathan helped Leah, her father, and her stepmother load a large farm wagon parked in front of the barber shop. When most of the household goods were packed, Nathan and Leah sat down on the wooden bench on the raised sidewalk. Light from the setting sun struck only the tops of the buildings on the east side of the street. There were no clouds in the sky. The daily breeze began to dwindle. The excitement of the day had died down, and only a few people could be seen on Main Street.

"I don't suppose Colin's daddy would want to come back and open the bank now that all the money's been recovered?" Leah questioned.

"Come back to what? Look at this, Leah. It's the summer that a town died."

"I guess it ain't much of a town, is it?"

"It's freezing cold in the winter, blistering hot in the summer. There's no trees, no grass, not much water that's fit to drink, and the wind blows every day of the year. It's a lousy place for a town."

"But we had some good times, didn't we, Nathan?"

"Yeah," he sighed. "That's what makes a place home. It's not the buildings or the location or the wind. It's the people. When the people you really like move away and all you've got left is a wood-frame house that leaks during a heavy storm, where marbles roll toward the fireplace . . ."

"I remember the first time I saw you." She smiled. "You crawled off that stage lookin' like an orphan calf."

"Me? How about you? Barefoot and wearing a dirty dress."

"It wasn't dirty," she protested. "I just . . . used it a lot."

"You were about the only one in town who would talk to me," Nathan replied.

"We were still livin' in the tent then," Leah added. "Daddy says he got us a nice house up on a hill in Austin."

"Everything in Pony Canyon is on a hill!" Nathan laughed.

"They got a good school, too. Daddy says I can either go to school or get me a job. I think maybe I'll try some more school. What are you going to do, Nathan?"

"I don't know. Mama said she might fill in teaching those kids that are left up here. There's always a chance we'll move to Austin, too. If Daddy ever became sheriff, then we could still be . . . uh . . . friends."

"Well, I'm goin' to pray every night that you move to Austin!" Leah stood up and stared across the street. "This is a crazy conversation," she announced. "It's like I'm up in the air staring down at us talkin'. It's just not real. It can't really be happenin'. This ain't the way I planned my life at all."

Nathan stood up and walked over by Leah. "Well, maybe it's the way the Lord planned it."

"If so, I don't think I like the plan," she said softly.

"Maybe not, but it's a better plan than if we'd never gotten to meet each other in the first place." Nathan turned his head toward the stairs. "I think your mother's calling you."

"My stepmother," Leah corrected him.

"I'd better go get my supper, too. What time you pulling out in the morning?"

"About sun-up, I guess." Leah turned to go up the stairs.

"I'll be over here on this bench at daybreak. You won't leave town without saying goodbye, will you?"

"Nathan T. Riggins, if you ain't over here to say goodbye in the mornin', I'll march up there and drag you out of bed in your nightshirt!"

"I'll be here." He laughed.

"Well, it's a good thing!" She grinned and ran up the stairs just like he had seen her do hundreds of times before.

■

Nathan climbed out of bed before daylight. It had been so warm during the night that he slept on top of the covers. After dressing and carrying in an arm load of wood, he scooted out the front door. Even though it was mostly dark, he stepped over to check on Tona. Then he remembered. Tears welled up in his eyes.

"Well, ol' boy . . . it's going to take me a while to get into a new routine. Now I don't have anyone left to really talk to—except maybe Onepenny."

He walked along the darkened street. The wind twirled dust in his face. There was no boom and vibration of the stamp mill, no shouts and shots from McGuire Street, no dogs barking, no roosters crowing, no kids playing tag on the sidewalks, no freight wagons circling the Mercantile.

Thanks, too, for Galena, Lord. I had a good time here. The history books won't ever remember it. But I will. I was here. And most of all, so were You.

■

Leah sat on the bench in front of the barber shop wearing her new dress.

"Mornin', Nathan."

"Mornin', pretty Miss Leah."

"Don't you go teasin' me!"

"I'm not," he replied, looking down at his boots.

"Maybe next time your daddy comes down to Austin, you can come with him," she suggested.

"Yeah, and . . . and you could come up and visit us. Mama said you could stay with us anytime."

"Sure, that would be fine, wouldn't it?"

"I'll write to you, Leah. You got to promise to write back."

"I will, but I told ya, you cain't make fun of my spellin'."

"I won't."

For several moments neither said anything.

"Nathan, what are you going to do today?" she finally asked.

"I don't know. Maybe I'll go for a ride on Onepenny."

"Out to Rabbit Springs?"

"No, I think I'll find a new place. Some place that I've never seen before. Some place where there aren't any memories. Memories can sure hurt sometimes."

"Boy, you can say that again," Leah agreed. "Well, here they come." She pointed to her father and stepmother toting a couple of large green valises.

Nathan walked Leah over to the wagon. She spun around and threw her arms around Nathan's neck and hugged him tight. "I don't want to let go!" she cried. Surprising himself, Nathan kissed her on the cheek next to the field of freckles. She pulled back with a wide smile on her face. Then he helped her climb into the wagon.

"Thank you, sir." She smiled.

He tipped his hat. "You're welcome, ma'am."

"It's like the last page in a book, ain't it, Nathan?"

"Yeah. One of those that you don't want to end, and you've been trying to read real slow so's to make it last."

The wagon started to roll south.

Leah looked frantic. Tears rolled down her cheeks.

"Cowboy!" she called. "You know I ain't never goin' to marry nobody but Nathan T. Riggins, don't ya?"

Nathan pushed his gray hat to the back of his head and waved to her.

"I know," he called back. He stared at the wagon until it pulled around the corner. Then he turned toward home and wiped his eyes on his dusty shirt sleeve.

Epilogue

TASHAWNA CHOLACH

At the age of eighteen, Tashawna joined BUFFALO BILL'S WILD WEST SHOW AND CONGRESS OF ROUGH RIDERS OF THE WORLD and made two tours of Europe as a trick rider. Returning to Carson City, Nevada, she became active in local theater productions. She married Colin Maddison, Jr., on July 4, 1895. They lived in a large home on the mountain just west of the city.

COLIN MADDISON, JR.

Majoring in business, Colin graduated from the University of California at Berkeley and then returned to Carson City, Nevada. At the age of twenty-five, he purchased the Ormsby State Bank. The bank was moderately successful. In 1903 he invested heavily in mining stock at Goldfield, Nevada. Selling out in 1905, Colin's profits were of legendary proportions, earning him the nickname "Lucky" Maddison. He and his wife (the former Tashawna Cholach) had one child, Colin Maddison III (with two *d*'s).

ONEPENNY

The talented spotted horse served Nathan (and his children) for thirty-two years. At one time it was the best-known horse in Lander County, Nevada. When Onepenny died, he was buried in the family grave site near the Salmon River in Idaho.

LEAH WALKER

Leah graduated from Nevada Normal and taught in a mission school in the Hawaiian Islands for two years. She then returned to the mainland and taught in rural schools in Nevada and Idaho for twenty-six years. Leah and her husband had six sons of their own and adopted three daughters. She contributed to the Federal Writers' Project on the History of Nevada and also to the project on the history of Idaho. She and Tashawna Maddison became the best of friends.

NATHAN TIMOTHY RIGGINS

Three days after Thanksgiving, Nathan and his parents moved to Austin, Nevada, where Mr. Riggins served as acting sheriff. Nathan received a one-year diploma at Mr. Dwight L. Moody's Bible School in Chicago, Illinois. He then took classes at Nevada College of Agriculture and Mining. In 1893 he married Leah Walker in Austin. It was estimated that 640 people attended the wedding. Soon after, Mr. and Mrs. Nathan Riggins moved to central Idaho where they formed Tona Land & Cattle Company and began a ranching career. The sprawling two-story white clapboard ranch house they built in 1902 is visible from U. S. Highway 95.

For a list of other books by STEPHEN BLY
or information regarding speaking engagements
write: Stephen Bly
           Winchester, Idaho 83555